ANNALISE HARDMAN

The Night of Two Moons

This book contains mild violence and romantic themes. It is intended for readers aged 16 and older.

First edition

ISBN: 978-1-0369-1237-6

This book was professionally typeset on Reedsy.
Find out more at reedsy.com

This book is dedicated to my amazing mum, who makes me believe in the magic of this story every single day.

Your unwavering support means everything to me.

Contents

Prologue

The moment something bad happens to you, your mind instinctively jumps to one question: *What did I do to deserve this?* That night, when I was ambushed, my brain spiralled through every terrible thing I'd done, every life I'd taken. I scrambled to think which vengeful family I had wronged, who might be coming for retribution. But as the Queen's assassin, the list of enemies was endless.

Chapter One

As soon as I stepped out of the tavern, I sensed bodies emerging from the shadows. In the next second, a sack was pulled over my head, the coarse material scraping against my cheeks and nose, and the world went black. Instinctively, I reached for the dagger forever tucked in my boot, but rough and calloused hands quickly pinned both arms behind my back - too quickly, as if they knew it was the first thing I would do. So instead, I thrashed wildly, tossing my body from side to side and bucking out behind me. My heart lifted as my foot connected with a tender male part, which was accompanied by a muffled groan.

I took the opportunity and yanked my hands free and backing away blindly. Straight into a solid mass. The fight drained from my body as I felt the cool kiss of a blade against my neck, a warning of the consequences if I pulled a move like that again. A silent threat I knew all too well.

I stilled instantly, straining to hear any sounds or voices from the dark depths inside the sack. I couldn't accurately make out how many ambushers there were. The sounds were too confused and muffled - just hurried whispers blending together. I guessed there were about three or four of them, but I couldn't be sure. The person behind me gripped my wrists in an iron hold, binding them tightly with rope until my skin chafed beneath it. With a rough shove, they pushed me forward.

I walked slowly, completely blinded, and my shin slammed painfully into a step in front of me. I stumbled upward, struggling to regain my balance, before being shoved again - this time into a carriage. I tumbled onto its plush seating, my body sinking into the soft cushions.

There was already a burly body at one end of the seat, and another slammed the door shut before wedging themselves beside me. I was sandwiched. Unable to attempt escape.

I wouldn't have bothered trying anyway, not when I was blindfolded.

There was a low shout from the front of the carriage, and I jolted in my seat as a horse let out a whinny, and it began to trundle along the uneven cobblestone streets. I sat rigidly upright, trying my hardest not to lean into the bodies on either side of me. My heart was pounding wildly against my ribcage. Perhaps this was my karma catching up to me. For all the lives I had claimed, now mine was being taken in exchange. A fair bargain I suppose. But my heart ached as I thought of my family, how they would react if I was killed - it would destroy them. I was their everything, and they were mine.

I needed to get out of here, for their sake more than my own.

Concentrate, I told myself. *You are a trained assassin. You can get out of here, but first you need to calm yourself down.*

With a shaky exhale I forced myself to close my eyes and take some deep breaths. I had to be smart. Aware. Using all my senses, seeing as my sight had been taken from me. All I could hear at the moment was some loud mouth-breathing from the ambusher to the left of me and the rain drumming its fingers against the roof of the carriage and splattering against the windows.

A small ember of hope burned in my chest. Surely if my ambushers wanted to kill me then they could have done it by now, and they hadn't? Why would they have gone through the effort of capturing me if they could have stabbed me the moment my hands were tied behind my back?

Unless they wanted to torture me first. The ember extinguished with a dull fizzle.

I needed to consider my options. I couldn't reach for my dagger again; I would be killed the second I tried. I also couldn't escape through the carriage windows with this damn sack over my head, as well as the fact I was utterly surrounded and outnumbered. The only option I had left was to let the ambushers take me wherever we were headed and try and talk it out with them. Convince them that killing people wasn't personal, it was my job. It was my duty to the Queen. To Nexonia.

* * *

When you are without one of your vital senses, time seems to elongate. It seemed like an eternity had passed before the carriage eventually came to an abrupt stop and I was lurched forward from my seat, caught at the last moment by those rough hands I was becoming all too familiar with. I was yanked from the carriage and a firm push told me to keep moving forward. I hesitated, my throbbing shin acting as a reminder of walking without being able to see where I was going, and once again I stumbled as my foot grazed an unseen step. I climbed carefully, tapping my toe in front of me to locate my next step, my movements slow and deliberate. All until another impatient shove struck me from behind.

'You know, I would move a lot quicker if I could see where I was going?' I hissed from under the sack. My blood was beginning to boil from being pushed about. I was met with no response. I huffed and carried on my ascent until I finally managed to reach the top of the many stairs without falling. My ears pricked at the sound of some soft murmurs and then the soft click of a door opening.

'Onwards,' the ambusher behind me barked, not pushing me this time. The air inside was warm and inviting compared to the biting chill of the wind and I followed the sound of footsteps marching along a lengthy corridor and finally into a large room. Hands pushed down on my shoulders until my knees buckled and I found myself sitting on a hard seat.

My family knew my routines well, they would definitely be panicking by now that I hadn't returned home.

A hand was placed on the sack, and I stiffened - waiting for some terrible blow to the skull - but instead, the sack was ripped off my head. I blinked in the sudden light. And then my jaw dropped.

Golden chandeliers scintillated from above, casting pearls of light against the matching golden walls, from which hung frowning portraits of a bloodline of royals. Before me sat a regal, solid gold throne, and upon the throne sat a golden Queen.

The Queen of Nexonia.

The very Queen I had served loyally for seven years, since I was just sixteen. The one I risked my life for every day as part of her small elite team of assassins, trained to eliminate any threat to her crown. The same Queen I continued to work for, even as my duties made me question what kind of sociopath I was becoming, every single day.

And yet despite all of this, I had never actually *met* her. I had laid eyes on her from afar as part of a crowd when she delivered her occasional speeches each year to the masses. But never, had I spoken to her in person, face to face.

And yet here she was in all her glory.

Long, pointed spikes erupted from the solid gold crown that nestled upon her blonde hair, braided and coiled tightly like snakes around her head. She had a face like butter - smooth and rich - undeniably beautiful.

But her eyes held none of that warmth.

They were steely grey in their sockets and cold as they settled upon me. My blood thickened in my veins, freezing like chunks of ice.

The Queen's eyes held so much power that I didn't even notice the struggling hostages beside her until a muffled cry shattered the silence of the room. My breath caught in my throat. There were two of them. Like me their wrist were also bound, but the sacks had not yet been removed from their heads. They wriggled like captured worms in their seats and my heart began to thud faster. Behind them stood a long line of twelve guards, all stood to attention, as still as statues, and coated in matching silver-plated armour. What in the Veil was going on here?

My attention returned to the Queen again. I opened my mouth to say something, of what, I wasn't quite sure, but the Queen of Nexonia spoke instead, her words slicing across my starting stutter.

'Young Aurora,' she said, her words as cold as those steel grey eyes, 'The girl I have heard so much about, in the flesh.'

5

My mouth went dry. She knew my name? She knew who I was? Before I could think of a reply the Queen continued.

'Excuse the methods of getting you here. We didn't want anyone to see you coming so thought it was best to get you here incognito.' She waved a hand impatiently, clearly knowing she should mention the unnerving methods she had employed to get me to the palace, but didn't deem it important to dwell on. I didn't realise I was gawking at her until her brows scrunched in disgust.

'It's- it's no problem, your Majesty,' I stammered.

'No doubt you are wondering why I have brought you here, Aurora. I have something very important that you must do for me.' She looked up then, her sharp eyes scanning the line of guards who stood to the side. 'Clear the room!' she snapped.

Immediately the guards turned and filed out, all but one who stayed put. We all waited in tense silence as they left, the Queen drummed her fingers against the arm of the throne until the door had closed and the sound of heavy footsteps died away down the corridor. With a deep breath, her eyes swivelled back to me. 'As I was saying, I have an important job for you. And you *will not* fail me.' She let a silence linger between us before she sniffed and raised her head. 'Bring in the Heir.'

The *Heir*. I could feel my pulse in my neck now. The Heir was the son of the Queen of Nexonia, destined to inherit the throne and rule the land after her reign ended. At just seven years old, he was rarely seen by the public as he was kept under strict protection, and it was only on the first day of each new year that he made a brief appearance by his mother's side to stare wide-eyed at the crowds, a rare and significant moment for our land.

A door that had been built into the wall opened behind the Queen's throne and to my confusion a mousy woman entered, struggling to carry a heavy bundle of sheets in her arms. I looked around her, trying to spot the Heir. I knew at seven years of age he should be perfectly able to walk by himself, and yet he was nowhere to be seen. That's when I spotted the small hand poking from the bundle. As the woman reached the throne I could see him now, the future King's face peeking out from under the sheets, and a gasp threatened in my throat.

He was so deathly pale that I could see every purple vein in his face, there were dark smudges under his closed eyes that gave him a haunted quality. Scarlet drops of blood stained the white sheets and I could hear every uneven breath he drew rattling in his chest. There was no doubt about it - he was dying. The Queen read every emotion that flickered across my face, and her nostrils flared.

'As you know, the Heir is *essential* to the stability and future of Nexonia. Since his father, our late King, has passed, and I am much too old now to bear another child, my son is my only hope. And without him to take over the throne, chaos will ensue. Without an Heir to take my place through blood, the throne by default, becomes available to anyone in my land. Without a doubt, a civil war will break out in its place of my position. With my land's best interest at heart, I cannot allow this to happen, there would be terrible death and destruction. I would shame my bloodline.' Her eyes strayed to the portraits of her predecessors on the wall, and she drew a sharp breath, rolling her shoulders as if she could ease the burdens that had been placed on them since she was born.

'The Heir is dying. I have tried everything to heal him over the past few weeks. Doctors, medicines, physicians. Nothing has worked. They can only tell me they think he has a serious case of Tuberculosis, but they are unable to help him and now time is running out.' I heard her swallow in the silence. 'It is predicted he will not last until the end of this week. So, something has to be done, *now*. And that's where you come in.'

She tore her eyes from the Heir, her son and only hope, to pin them on me. A lump lodged its way into my throat. She was right, if the Heir died then there wouldn't be a man or woman in Nexonia who wasn't fighting to the death for her place in ruling. But how could I help? I knew some basic medical training, dressing simple wounds and such, but *this* was very much not my area of expertise.

'I have been racking my brain for the past few weeks on what I could do to save my boy, as well as Nexonia, and I have come up with a solution. It is not something I *ever* wanted to do, but I have no other option. I spoke to

General Ambrose, the leader of my assassin team as I am sure you are aware, and I asked him who he thought would be best suited for my mission. Not just the toughest person in his squad, but also the fastest, the sneakiest, and the most intelligent. And he chose you.' The Queen's gaze hardened on me, her eyes searching my face for fear, yet she found none and so continued. I was much too numbed by shock to be scared right now. 'So, Aurora, you will take the Heir tomorrow night, the Night of Two Moons, across the Veil into the Fae Land.'

The whole world narrowed to that one word. *Fae*. The room was enveloped in a deadly silence. Even the hostages stopped wriggling in their seats. The guard behind them flinched. My head emptied.

'You- you want me to go to the *Faeries?*' I repeated dumbly. The Queen's face darkened; her fingers digging into the gold upholstery of the throne. I could hear her teeth grinding from across the room as she heaved another deep, tired breath.

'That is what I said. It is not the option I ever wanted to resort to, but it is my last and only hope of keeping him alive. As I mentioned, tomorrow night is the Night of Two Moons, and the Veil between our land and the Fae's will open for an hour. You will enter into the Fae Land with the Heir and find the Fae, and then you will strike a bargain with them. You must find something we can offer them in exchange for them healing the Heir - whatever it is they want, whether it be our best soldiers or our finest entertainers. Whatever it is, you *must* get them to agree to heal the Heir. It is imperative you do not fail. Do you understand?'

I understood all right. I understood she was sending me to the lion's den. And I was just a lamb in comparison to them, their power. It didn't matter if I was the best killer in Nexonia, the Fae could squash me like a bug with their power without a second thought.

My voice sounded foreign, far away, as I spoke, 'Are you sure this is wise? Do you really think the Fae will even listen to me if I tried to bargain with them?'

The Queen's eyes flared. 'We have no other options! Do you think I would go to *them* if there were another choice? It is my responsibility to look after this land and I will not let down my bloodline. I have to try.

'The Heir has but mere days left, so if there is *anything* we can offer them in exchange for his health, then we must. Now, you are to go tomorrow night and be waiting by the Veil before the moons collide and the hour begins. You will be accompanied by my most trusted guard, Sylas.'

She raised her chin to the one remaining guard in the room. 'I will not be sending any other guards with you, as the Fae may see this as a threat, and I am certain my people will grow concerned if they realise I have sent all my best soldiers off to the Fae Land. They may tell their families where they are going, and people will start to talk. I cannot afford to lose them. So, you two will go and do everything in your power to save the Heir. Sylas will meet you there tomorrow night with the Heir.'

My thoughts scrabbled to reach my mouth. 'But surely - surely they might just reject the offer of a bargain and kill the Heir, as well as ourselves, right there and then?'

The Queen closed her eyes and pinched the bridge of her nose. She suddenly seemed old and tired. 'I know that this is a possibility. But I have had to make my peace with it. If they do not help him, then he will die anyway, regardless of whether it's by their hand or by his illness. At least this way there is a sliver of hope. As for you, think of it as a sacrifice for Nexonia.'

I was struck dumb. My mouth worked but no sound came out. I could not believe I was being sent directly into the Fae Land; the one place that had been drilled into me since birth to never go near. And now I was not only to enter, but try and make a deal with the Fae. Only a few people in history had ever crossed into Fae territory on the Night of Two Moons. None had ever come back. That was warning enough.

I thought of having to tell my family what I had been asked to do when I returned home tonight, seeing their horrified faces as they knew it would likely be the last time they ever saw me alive.

'Oh, you won't need to explain this to your family,' the Queen sneered, as though she had read my thoughts. 'They heard every word.'

She took her time to walk from the throne to the hostages. She reached a hand and snatched the sack of each off their heads. All the air left my lungs.

With eyes wide and black tape across their mouth to stifle any complaint, my beloved Ma and Pa sat, bound to their chairs. My whole body went into numb shock. Anger roared in my ears, that cunning evil b-

'I thought you might need a little incentive to get the job done. You bring the Heir back healthy; your family walks free. You fail, your family dies.'

Chapter Two

My home felt cold and lifeless without my parents' presence. This had been my safe place. The minute I entered the front door I was no longer a ruthless, trained assassin - I was a *daughter*. I was *loved*. I was *protected*. This was the place where the blood, the killing, the trauma from the day melted away as I sat in front of the crackling fire, laughing and eating with my family.

I stared ahead at the unlit hearth now. There had been no laughter nor happiness when I returned to the empty house last night. The only sound in this place was my own breath, clouding in front of me as I stood in the chilled hallway. I couldn't help but wonder where my parents had been forced to sleep last night, what disgusting dungeon they might be rotting in at this very moment. For them, I had to succeed. For them, I had to bring the Heir back alive and healthy.

With that thought, I snatched my cloak from the stand and slammed the door shut behind me without looking back. I stepped out onto the streets, shrugging the cloak over my shoulders to shield me from the nipping winds. I chucked a glance each way before turning left and stalking down the darkened streets. As I walked, I felt a deep burning fury writhing in my chest. I had spent my life dedicated to serving the Queen, *killing* for her, and this was my payment? Holding my family hostage until I completed a mission almost certain to end in my death?

Clomping hooves coming from behind brought me out of my miserable thoughts and I tucked myself into the doorway of a house so the horse and carriage could move past. The further I walked, the narrower and dirtier the streets became. These houses were closer to Fae territory, occupied by the poorest of the poor. The ones who couldn't afford to be further away. Filth lined the streets, rats scuttled about the newspapers discarded on the floor, babies cried out amidst the cursing and shouting that could be heard through the thin walls on either side of me. But the streets themselves were eerily empty today, as they always were on this night each month. The Night of Two Moons. The night when instead of one moon, there were two, and they inched closer together until at midnight they collided. For that hour, the Veil between our land and the Fae's opened. People always locked themselves away early on this night - not that the Fae ever came across to our side. Throughout the centuries we humans had been the ones to cross over, not them. But people locked themselves away - just in case.

I stole a glance at the brief snatch of sky that could be seen between the crowded heads of the houses on either side of me. The moons were creeping closer - I didn't have long. I quickened my pace as I slipped through the shadows, and I soon reached the end of the street, where the houses and cobblestone just stopped abruptly, as if afraid to take a step closer to the Fae territory.

I paused, my foot hovering between the space where the cobblestone ended and the grass began. Just ahead of me, a bridge stretched over a raging river, and then I would have to cross a wide, hilly field before I got to the stretch of forest, in which the Fae lurked. As instructed by the Queen, I did a thorough check over my shoulder to ensure nobody was watching me, which of course they weren't, as nobody ever went past this point, especially not on this night.

I rolled my neck, letting it crack in its socket. *Come on, Aurora, you can do it.* With slow uncertainty, I allowed my boot to make contact with the grass - past the point most people in Nexonia would ever cross in their lifetime. I couldn't look back now. I hurried along the bridge, each slat complaining under the weight of my heavy boots. Underneath, the river frothed and foamed. I crossed to the other side and started up the hill. The air was so fresh out here, so different from the sewage and sickness that polluted the poorer ends of Nexonia.

The dewy grass underfoot was slick and I almost tumbled back to the bottom of the hill multiple times before I managed to stagger to the top, by which time I was sweating profusely despite the soft spits of rain. I threw back my cloak hood, releasing my fiery red hair to tumble from its bounds, and squeezing my eyes shut as I tilted my head to the sky.

I wondered for a moment if this was all… some kind of nightmare, that I might open my eyes in a moment and find I was still tucked in my bed at home, my parents safely tucked in their own room across the hall from me.

But the cool droplets of water running down my cheeks and down the inside of my collar, making me shudder, were certainly real. I opened my eyes again, and down below was the dark line of forest against the blue-grey stained sky. The place where our land ended and the Fae's began. A shiver teased its way down my spine.

A small flash of silver below snatched my attention and I spotted Sylas waiting by the tree line in his full armour - steel cuirass and close helm, dark blue tabard, thick sturdy boots, and a sword sheathed at his side. His tall, and rather intimidating build, was made even more so by the tiny bundle of sheets he held in his arms. The Heir. I made my way toward him, every step I took toward the Fae Land and away from my own - away from my parents - was heavy with dread. Yet, I dragged one foot in front of another until I stood right before Sylas, staring up at him. He didn't even bother to acknowledge me; he was too busy staring up at the sky as the two moons began to slowly merge together. I was surprised he could even see with that helmet on, which granted him only a slim slice of vision. But I supposed it was wise of him to wear it to cover his identity, and I secretly wished I had one too.

But on the other hand, I guess it didn't matter in the end; it was highly likely we would get killed the minute we entered the Fae Land so a helmet wouldn't be much help. I peered at the bundle in Sylas's arms. I could see the Heir up close now, and I recoiled at the sight of him. He looked so shrivelled and frail, as helpless as a baby. The only indication he was sleeping rather than dead was the wheezing sound escaping from his parted lips. My heart went out to him. No child deserved to suffer like this. I decided to shift my gaze to the moons instead, waiting silently as they slid into place, two becoming one. Behind us there was a soft hiss, and I turned as a translucent wall stretching the whole distance of the forest rippled slightly and then disappeared.

The Veil was down.

Our hour started now - an hour to find the Fae, try and strike a bargain with them, not get killed, *and* be out before the moons passed each other and we were trapped in the Fae Land until the next Night of Two Moons in a month's time.

The entrance into the forest was clear. The only way to enter the thick tangle of wooden limbs was through a hollow tunnel created from crippled trees that bent at odd angles, allowing us to pass through into the heart of the forest. A daring invitation.

'Let's go.' I jumped at the sound of Sylas's low voice coming from behind the helmet. He didn't waste any time as he set off first through the entrance. I dithered, stealing one last longing glance back in the homeward direction before following up the rear.

We weren't far into the tunnel when the light began to fade; the silvery moonlight choked off by the long, gnarled fingers of trees clasped overhead. Neither Sylas nor I spoke as we moved through, ears pricking at every twig that crunched underfoot as we infiltrated deeper and deeper into the Fae Land. The trees braided overhead often stooped low, pressing in on me as if trying to hear the traitorous pounding of my heart. Brambles clawed at my cloak, warning me it wasn't too late to turn back.

I had no idea where the Faeries lived, only that they resided somewhere within these tangled depths. In Nexonia, everyone's beliefs about Fae came from tall rumours or from creepy books that told embellished tales of Fae with five heads and sharpened claws, which I hoped by the Veil wasn't true. But one common rumour was that you knew you were getting closer to their territory when a strong sense of dread settled in your gut. And if you had the nerve to follow that horrid feeling, it would lead you right to them. However, I'd been feeling uneasy ever since I left my house tonight, so I wasn't sure how helpful that apparent sensation would be to me if the rumour was true.

We finally exited the tunnel of trees, which opened up to a daunting forest. It was so still. So quiet. The trees here were bare and twisted - ugly - with huge roots that crawled along the ground. I jumped as a crow swooped past, landing on the thick arm of a tree, cocking its sleek head to one side so it could watch us through its beady, button-like eye. Sylas stared at it for a good long while before taking off through the forest.

'Where are you going? You can't just walk off, we need to stick together,' I hissed after him, hating that I was bound to him for the rest of the night. I was always sent on my assassin missions' solo, because that's how I worked best. Alone. But Sylas held the Heir, so I couldn't abandon him. Once again, I was ignored, and he marched straight on with a sense of urgency. I made a rude gesture to his back.

The further we walked, the more I noticed the temperature dropping rapidly. My joints began to feel stiff; my fingers were cramping up badly, but I didn't dare put them in my pockets. It was crucial to be on guard at all times. We had to be ready if caught unaware.

I opened my mouth to hiss at Sylas again - when it hit me. The feeling the legends had talked about. Like a cold dripping sensation spreading through my body, within my very veins, infiltrating every thought and feeling. Dread. Dread like I had never felt it before. Taking a hold of me like a curse. It was so all-consuming that it was an effort to remember how to walk and I just stood there, shaking. Terrible thoughts started polluting my mind; thoughts of my parents being tortured and killed if we didn't succeed, thoughts of the Heir cold and lifeless. My eyes traced the ground, stopping as they took in something small and sharp, buried in the undergrowth. Was that - a *bone*?

'Come on, we need to keep moving,' Sylas's impatient tone tugged me back to my senses. I snapped my head up. He was standing across from me, staring down as I shook uncontrollably. *Get it together, Aurora. Your family are relying on you.*

I managed to drag one foot in front of the other and we kept going. I felt thoroughly rattled from the experience, the sudden spiralling of thoughts that I fell surrender to. If the rumour of feeling dread when you are nearby the Fae was true, then that might mean...

15

'I think we are close,' I breathed to Sylas, my finger pointing toward the low-lying green mist that slithered along the forest floor up ahead. Beyond that, the earth rose into a high, dirt-packed mound that shut out the rest of the forest like a wall. The mist seemed to be ebbing from a source behind the earthy barrier. Every inch of my body was screaming at me to turn back now. But I just kept walking forward, until that mist licked at my boots, flowing around me like a river.

As we advanced on the mound, sounds became clearer. A low symphony of humming and hissing was coming from the other side that sent chills snaking down my back. I looked over to Sylas who confirmed my suspicions with a nod - the Fae territory was on the other side.

We scrambled up, it was so steep we had to clamber on our hands and knees, I dug my fingers deep into the dirt and beside me Sylas did the same, but with only one hand as his other held the Heir. We reached the top and I dared to peek over. My dread melted into awe. It was spectacular.

Along the forest floor were homes, shops, stalls, all constructed from earthly materials; wood, moss, leaves. But the buildings didn't stop there, they climbed trees, nestled in the broad tree branches, or even within the trees themselves. Circular windows had been carved into the hollow trunks, within soft light flickered. Between the trees were a tangle of bridges, constructed from wood and held together with a silvery thread that winked in the strands of moonlight filtering through the canopy above. Fireflies the size of birds hummed as they drifted along, bathing the place in a warm, otherworldly glow.

And amongst all this, there were Fae everywhere. Each looked unique to the next, not a single one the same. Some were frightful, with grotesquely grey or blue skin, wide ribcages, protruding black veins lining their body. Others were radiant, beauty in abundance with their long, flowing hair and perfectly crafted faces. I noticed some even had animalistic features; hooved feet, wings, tails, horns. But they were all exceedingly tall with elongated limbs that would have meant they towered above even the tallest human in Nexonia. Their clothing bore similar shades to their surroundings - greens, and browns, and blacks - and they were loose on the body, floating in an invisible breeze.

'It's rude to stare, you know?' A sinister snarl coming from my right had me jumping back, clamping my lips together to stop the scream escaping. I whirled around to see two dark pools of infinite black staring into my soul. The Fae's ribcage was so tight against his stretched pale skin I was worried it might burst at any moment, and his face was cruel, split into a wicked smile to broadcast every pointed tooth crammed into his mouth.

I was tough. I was an excellent fighter and an even better killer. But when that *thing* licked its lips with a bulging tongue as it studied my every move, everything I knew about myself went to shit. His words were slimy in his mouth. 'It's been some time since I last saw a human, especially one so pretty. Such a shame.'

A long, spindly finger uncoiled and reached for me, his nail carved a line down my cheek, and I felt warm blood trickle down my face. The air was filled with the metallic tang of blood - my blood - and the black of the Fae's eyes widened.

He was going to eat me.

'We are here to speak to the Fae Queen,' Sylas's voice interrupted. The Fae's attention snapped to him, his face contorting with anger, but Sylas continued, 'I don't think she would be pleased if you kill us before she hears what we have to say. We have been sent by the Queen of Nexonia personally.'

The Fae ground his teeth. I didn't move as its eyes flicked between us, considering what it was going to do. And as much as Sylas had been blunt and a pain in the ass to me so far, I was so grateful the Queen had sent him along with me. Else I would have been eaten alive before even getting the chance to speak to the Fae Queen. The Fae returned his gaze to me, lingering on the blood-stained cheek hungrily.

'Very well. I will take you to Queen Velraxis,' he snarled. 'It's your funeral.'

Chapter Three

I felt eyes from all directions prickling into me as the Fae led us through
the land, into the heart of their territory. Cold, curious, hungry
eyes. The Fae stared unblinkingly, their eyes tracking our every move.
Whatever they had been doing previously was forgotten, their curiosity
piqued. Some stopped mid-flight, fluttering down to the ground to inspect
us, others leaned over the bridge over-head to get a better look, their faces
glowing in the soft twilight. The vibrant chatter now became pointed
whispers behind our backs.

I refused to look anywhere but the pale ribbed back of the Fae leading us
in front. Despite being hideous, he moved with ethereal grace, his long limbs
moving easily as he strode toward an enormous tree at the end of the stretch
of buildings. This particular tree was double the length of my home and
thrice the height. It towered above us, its branches reaching for the synched
moons above. Its trunk was fully covered with delicate carvings of winged
creatures, insects, patterns, all woven in different scenes together, so tiny
that it must have taken hundreds of years to complete.

Built into the tree were two broad oak doors, guarded by a pair of stone-
faced guards. Each had their fingers wrapped around sharpened staffs and
bore matching black armour that displayed their bulging muscles. By the
scars littered across their bodies that spoke of countless fights - that they
had emerged from victorious - they were not someone you wanted to cross.
This was clearly the Fae Queen's palace.

The Fae leading us stopped before the set of stairs that led up to those double doors.

'Wait here,' he barked to me. He approached the guards and spoke to them in hushed tones, turning once to point a wicked finger at Sylas and I who stood silently side by side. The Heir heaved a cough within his sheets. One of the guards nodded and slipped inside, leaving the Fae wringing his hands as he waited.

Time dilated as we all stood there. I held my head high and clutched my hands together to stop them from shaking. I wasn't used to feeling weak. I was used to being the most powerful, the most deadly, in the room. But in this territory, I was nothing. In my peripheral vision I could feel Faeries gathering around us, and I dared a glance over my shoulder. Fae were crowding around, jostling one another to get the best view of the humans bold enough to enter this land. I couldn't help but notice they looked… nervous. Their gazes were wide as they shifted to each other, they whispered behind long-limbed hands, nudging one another and shaking their heads. Why were they anxious - they had more power in their pinkie than I had in my whole body? I saw one female Fae drag her child from the front of the crowd and instead put herself in front as a shield.

And then something changed.

I felt her before I saw her. I turned back to face the steps just as the air crackled with something dark. Imposing. Unforgiving. Black mist leaked down the wooden steps. In unison, all the Fae dropped to one knee, a palm to their forehead.

And there she was, Queen Velraxis. The Fae Queen.

Thick ebony hair cascaded to her waist; two braided strands fell in front of her pointed ears. Huge jewels embellished her fingers, a shade too black to exist in the mortal realm. She moved like a shadow, barefoot under the midnight dress that floated around her, ending in thin smoky tendrils. My breath snagged at the sight of her eyes. There was no pupil - they were two pits of fire that had no start or end. I could feel them as hot as coals upon my face as she surveyed me.

A rustle of feathers and a squawk disturbed the unnerving silence that had descended as a crow swooped through the air and settled on her shoulder. It examined us with an eye. I had a strong feeling it was the same crow that had watched us earlier when we first entered the forest. The crowd of Fae hadn't moved nor spoken, still on their knees for their Queen. Now I understood why they were so nervous. Although the other Fae were no doubt powerful, the Queen's presence was *different*. Darker.

Worse.

'Stand,' she drawled, and they did so. My face blistered as her eyes roved from Sylas to me. 'Humans in my land. My, my, how long has it been?' She asked nobody in particular. Every word she spoke snaked around me, tightening my chest.

Sylas took a brave step forward, the bundle of sheets clutched tightly to his chest.

'We are here on behalf of the Queen of Nexonia. We are here to make a bargain with you,' he said thickly from under the helmet.

The Queen studied him, the armour, the Heir in his arms. I was surprised her stare alone didn't burn the metal right off of him. A smile carved her beautifully wicked face, the most unnerving thing she could have done in that moment.

'Your human Queen wishes to make a bargain, with me?' she mused. 'Your Queen thinks that *I* would ever help her out. How *interesting*,' she spat. My stomach contracted inside of me. I might as well use my dagger to slit my throat now, it would be kinder than any death she might impose upon us.

But Sylas wasn't giving up. He tugged the blanket down so the Heir's face was no longer covered but in clear view for the Fae Queen to see. 'This is the Heir to our throne. He plays a crucial part in our land, but he is dying, and we are out of options. Our Queen sent us here to see if there is anything we can do or offer you in exchange for you healing our Heir. We can offer you our best army troops, or finest dancers, or-'

'You mortals, think *you* can offer *us* something that we cannot obtain ourselves?' Queen Velraxis threw back her head then and cackled, the sound rich and terrifying. Some of the other Fae joined in with their Queen and the air filled with mocking laughter. Like nails down a chalkboard. I wanted it to stop, stop, stop-

'Surely there must be something?' I raised my voice over the noise. The laughter echoed around the space before it died away. The Queen's smile dropped as she beheld me, her eyes two pools of molten lava. I felt that burning sensation on my face again. I cleared my throat. 'There must be something we can give or do for you. Anything.'

The Queen clucked her tongue before pointing a finger at Sylas. 'You are clearly one of the human Queen's cronies.' Her gaze shifted back to me. 'So, who are you? What is your purpose?'

'I'm nobody,' I said truthfully. 'I am only here to try and make a bargain with you. The Queen of Nexonia is holding my family hostage until we return from here with the Heir healthy. If I fail, she will kill my parents. So, I ask you again, Queen Velraxis, surely there is *something* that someone *even* as powerful as yourself must desire.'

The cards were on the table. I wasn't foolish enough to expect her to pity me, or to help heal the Heir for mine or my parents' sake. But I needed her to see that we weren't hiding anything. Our motives were laid bare. What we wanted and what was at stake for us was painfully clear - and we were willing to do anything to get her help. My words fell into a pit of silence. The Queen stroked a spindly finger over the crow on her shoulder. I thought she might never speak again, that I would stand here and wither away whilst she took her time to think through my question. Even the forest held its breath.

'There is something. One thing I want,' she said slowly, thinking through her every word. Her eyes gleamed for a beat as she beheld us. But then she shook her head. 'But there isn't a chance in the Abyss a pair of mere mortals like yourselves could get it for me.'

But she had dangled the bait now and I pounced. 'Why not give us a chance? Queen Velraxis, you have *everything* to gain and we have *everything* to lose.'

The Fae surrounding us were silent, desperate to catch every word exchanged.

The Queen stilled. Her eyes narrowed on me, taking in the determined clench of my jaw, my knuckles cracking at my side. The weight of the offer seemed to hang in the air. Nobody spoke. Nobody moved. My muscles felt so tight with tension I thought they might burst.

'It's an object that I want. It's called the Divinal Stone,' the Queen said at last. Immediately a ripple of whispers flared through the place like a ripping wind. Sylas's free hand went straight to his sword, but the Queen merely held up a hand and the noise died instantly.

'Okay,' I urged, not wanting to lose the deal. 'What is this Divinal Stone, where can we find it?'

The Queen scowled at me, my eagerness. 'It's not that easy, girl.' She stopped suddenly, surveying the crowd of Fae leaning in to catch every word we exchanged. 'I think it's best we discuss this matter inside.'

She turned and strode into the palace, leaving us blinking in her sudden absence. The ugly Fae who had led us to the palace growled and jerked his head for us to follow him inside. We both made our way hesitantly up the steps, past the snarling guards and through the double doors which were closed behind us with a slam - shutting out the rest of the Fae.

The inside was a reflection of Queen Velraxis herself; dark and beautiful. The bark walls mirrored the intricate carvings of the exterior, their surfaces covered with drawings and symbols that I swore shifted subtly out the corner of my eye. From the high ceiling, gnarled roots dangled like chandeliers, intertwined with clusters of softly glowing mushrooms that bathed the room in a dim lighting. Queen Velraxis's molten eyes burned like embers at the other end of the room, where she lounged upon her throne. She traced a pointed nail along its dark, polished arm-rest.

Sylas and I approached cautiously but stopped at a respectful distance. The air itself felt alive, saturated with a heady mix of earthy dampness and an intoxicating floral perfume.

The Queen watched us carefully before continuing. 'As I was saying, the Divinal Stone is an ancient relic of immense strength, passed down through every Fae King or Queen for centuries. The Stone itself is the *essence* of power, possessing it, or even being in close proximity to it, increases our Fae abilities. We wear it as a symbol of our reign, but more importantly, it regulates and strengthens the magic of our land. Without it, our power wanes, gradually but inevitably. As Queen, I should possess it - but it was stolen from me, and without it, our magic as a whole weakens. I want what is *mine.* She spat the last word with such force that I flinched.

The Queen flexed her fingers before continuing. 'Queen Merida was my predecessor - up until fifty years ago, when she... lost her touch. Merida had always been wise and sensible, a friend to me, but then it all went wrong. A human priest from the Untamed Territory came into our land, claiming to be a psychic and demanding to talk to Merida. Whatever lies he fed her, whatever twisted visions he claimed to see about our land, they drove Merida mad. She became *obsessed* with some shadowy creature he had mentioned. She never gave us the full details, but she believed this creature was coming to destroy her reign.

'Merida started going to the Untamed Territory more and more, I don't know what she was working on with this priest, but I got the impression they were creating some kind of a weapon, something she believed would destroy this shadow figure.'

Queen Velraxis's eyes flashed with disdain. 'Merida was spending all her time in the Untamed Territory rather than her own land, abandoning her Queenly duties, and neglecting all of us Fae. She was slipping into insanity, haunted by the priest's visions. She wasn't fit to rule anymore. So, I had to make a hard decision. I decided that I would step up and take the throne. I gathered support and eventually confronted Merida to tell her that the Fae wanted me as their new ruler.

'I asked her *nicely* to hand over the Stone, but of course she refused. She became violent, and she and her remaining loyal followers attacked me, but fortunately, my supporters outnumbered hers, and we managed to defeat her.'

Something dangerous writhed in the depths of the Queen's eyes. 'But before she could die properly, Merida and her loyal followers made one final, selfish act. They sacrificed their lives to keep the Divinal Stone from me, ensuring I could never access its power. They combined their souls into a single monstrous entity - something we Fae have named the Shadow Warden. The very creature the priest had warned her about, the monster she had feared all this time, turned out to be herself. They cast a curse on the Stone: no Fae can touch it now, not unless a human willingly hands it over.

If we try to take it by force, the Stone will destroy itself. I cannot risk that.'

I couldn't help but ask, 'But why? Why would she curse it so that only humans could touch it?'

'Because,' Queen Velraxis snapped, growing impatient with my questions, 'humans fear us. They would never willingly help us. The curse ensures that we can't take the Stone back by force - it has to be given willingly to us. Merida thought that no human would ever agree to that.'

'So you want us to get you this Stone? Do you know where we would find it?'

'Merida and her followers - the Shadow Warden - took the Stone far north, into the Untamed Territory. There, they guard it with their very souls. I am unaware of their exact location.'

I felt my heart sink. 'But how are we supposed to defeat something like that?'

The Queen's eyes gleamed coldly. 'That is not my problem. You asked what I wanted, and that is it. If you find the weapon that Queen Merida and the priest created, you may be able to use it against the Shadow Warden.'

'But what if we don't find it?'

I could feel the Queen's frustration radiating like heat from her body. Her voice dripped with hatred. 'That, again, is not my concern. If you wish to back out of our bargain, I'm more than happy to send your body back to your Queen... along with a note of explanation.'

My throat tightened, and I swallowed hard. 'No. We'll do it.'

But my heart was sinking, all the hope drained from it. The weapon and the Divinal Stone were both in the Untamed Territory - the region beyond the Fae Land. It was a free-for-all. We knew humans lived out there, scattered about in villages. And in that land, horrible beasts and spirits roamed. Unimaginable terrors lay ahead.

But this was my only lifeline.

The Queen picked at her long nail. 'Well, there's our bargain. You go to the Untamed Territory, find the weapon, kill the Shadow Warden, and bring the Divinal Stone back to me. Once a human presents it to me, the curse will finally be broken, and I can access its power again. Then, and only then, will you get your Heir back, alive and healthy.'

I rubbed my forehead, trying to make sense of it all. 'Our Queen expected us back tonight, and we can't possibly hope to accomplish all of this in the slim window of time that we have left.'

The Queen flexed her knuckles. 'You are correct, this will take time. I will grant you one month. You have until the next Night of Two Moons to return with the Divinal Stone. I will sustain the Heir until then. But if you don't return, or come back without the Stone, your precious Heir dies.'

With a snap of her fingers, a roll of parchment appeared in her hand, black swirling writing curling across the page. She took her time to roll it up, never breaking the tether of eye contact, and raised it to her shoulder. The crow grasped it in its beak and took flight. It headed straight for me and I just managed to duck at the last second as it swooped past, escaping through a small hole carved in the bark.

'That parchment details our agreement. If your Queen signs it, the deal is sealed. I've made it clear - she'll have to wait until the next Night of Two Moons, as we discussed, to get her Heir back.'

I bobbed my head. But there was one significant question burning on my tongue. Queen Velraxis seemed to sense this, and her gaze hardened as though she could extract it from me with a single look. She gave me a serpentine grin. 'You're wondering how you can trust us?'

I nodded with all the bravery I could muster. What would stop her from killing the Heir, or me, the minute we handed her the Divinal Stone?

The Queen stood then, coming closer. Shadows curled at her feet. It took everything in me to not shrink away. Her smile was nothing short of a threat as she said, 'Why don't I show you how we Fae like to keep our word?'

Without looking back, she beckoned forth the Fae that brought us here, the one that had nearly eaten me without a second thought. His eyes widened in alarm, threatening to pop from their sockets. As he approached warily, his knees began to shake and buckle. It was so strange, to see something so grotesque and terrifying now quivering like a child before its mother.

The Queen smiled sweetly at him, 'I would like to show...' I felt the burn of her eyes on me.

I swallowed. 'Aurora.'

'I would like to show our friend Aurora and the human Queen's guard here, what happens when we Fae break our promises.'

Tears began to fall down his wicked face, but I couldn't find it in my hardened heart to feel sorry for him. The animosity on his face was draining away.

'Now, face Aurora and place a hand to your head.'

'Queen Velraxis, please, I beg-'

'IT'S AN ORDER!' Her words struck with such power that even I felt their weight, as if they could fold me in half like a fragile piece of parchment. The Fae's knees had buckled as the very ground beneath our feet trembled with the Queen's fury. He scrambled to his feet, stopping before me. Hatred burned in his eyes as he placed a hand to his forehead.

'Now you, Aurora,' the Queen said. Sylas took a step forward as if to stop the events, but I shook my head at him. I placed my palm to my forehead. 'Now I want you to make Aurora a false promise. Tell her that you aren't afraid of me.'

The Fae's lips quivered. 'Please-'

'If I have to ask you again, I will ensure your death is so slow and agonising that you will beg for me to end your suffering. I will peel the very skin from your body and let your organs fall one by one from your limp, disgusting body.' Her voice was honeyed now, which made the threat of a death sentence all the more horrifying. 'Now, tell the girl you are not afraid.'

'I- I am not afraid of Queen Velraxis,' he whispered. Immediately, his face drained of colour, and he became almost translucent. I could see every pumping organ in his body working away under that thin layer of skin, and then, just like that - they stopped. His eyes misted over, becoming unseeing, and his legs gave out from underneath him. He crumpled to the ground before me. Everything went still. There was no blood, no gore - he was just... dead. His wings gave a final reflexed twitch.

The Queen admired her handiwork with a pointy smile. Then her eyes returned to me. 'See how our promises work? If a Fae makes a Binding Promise, we stick to it. Or die.'

I dragged my eyes away from the lifeless body before me. I am an assassin; I have taken many lives. But *always* with purpose. I am only instructed to hunt those who are a threat to the Queen's ruling, to Nexonia. I am skilled, sneaky, and quick, and I try to ensure my kills are so swift that they are practically painless. And although killing is my job, I often feel it's just an identity I assume during the day, and I shed that skin by night. I try to feel indifferent about it - the killing - although there have been some awful nights when it all comes crashing down on me.

But this… this was different. The Queen was so cold, so unbothered by the death she commanded. She found it *amusing*. A flapping of wings sliced through the stillness of the air, startling me. The crow was back and settled again upon the Queen's shoulder as she extracted the contract from its beak.

She unrolled it, the pupilless eyes sweeping across the parchment, before announcing, 'Your Queen has agreed to my terms.' A curling smile distorted her face once again. 'Let's make our Binding Promises to one another then, Aurora.'

I took a deep breath, my lungs filling with that intoxicatingly sweet, earthy scent, and I began to move toward her. Sylas reached out to grab my arm, but with a casual wave, the Queen sent him stumbling away from me, propelled by nothing but air.

'Don't interrupt,' she snarled, eyes flaring. I forced myself to walk right up to her, my neck craning to meet that withering stare.

Up close, she was even more beautiful, even more terrifying. Power radiated off her in palpable waves. If she was this powerful without the Divinal Stone, then with it… the thought was unimaginable. From here her scent wrapped around me: a metallic tang, like burnt iron mingled with a seductive fragrance of night-blooming jasmine. There was a faint undertone of something else, something dark and elusive that I couldn't quite place - and didn't want to.

She put her hand to her forehead, the black jewels on her fingers winking at me in the dim lighting, and I copied the movement.

'Once you have presented the Divinal Stone to me, I will give you back your Heir alive and healthy. You will leave my land unharmed, as promised.

Once you've crossed back through the Veil, however, my oath no longer binds me.'

I felt cold snaking through my veins as the promise sealed. Sylas watched behind the depths of his helmet. I backed away, feeling as though I could breathe again now that there was distance between the Queen and I. Her gaze flicked to the Heir curled up inside the blankets within Sylas's arm. The Queen merely had to point, and the bundle of sheets was carried on an invisible wind, right into her arms. The movement made the Heir cough, a horrific gargling sound of blood. Queen Velraxis didn't so much as flinch at the sound of it, nor look concerned. The fact she could heal this poor, sick child with the snap of her fingers yet chose to make us endure unimaginable torment, filled me with rage. Her eyes burned into us one last time, a gaze that could break bones and set the forest ablaze without a second thought.

'You best get going then. Act fast, as though your lives depend on it. Because they do.'

With that, she turned and exited through an archway.

In her wake she left death and fear.

Chapter Four

I t was a fool's bargain, I knew that. Death was almost certain. But there wasn't another option. I had to die trying - I wouldn't be able to live with myself if I failed to save the Heir and my parents got killed.

Sylas and I had been guided around the back of the tree palace to wait for further instructions, and I was grateful to be relieved from the presence of Queen Velraxis. I picked at my thumb until it bled as we stood in tense silence. We were to head off tonight, as the journey was expected to be long and treacherous, and we would need as much time as possible if we wanted to be back by the next Night of Two Moons. It gave us but a month to try and locate the weapon that Merida and the priest had created, then find where the Shadow Warden was guarding the Divinal Stone, defeat the Shadow Warden, and also bring the Stone back with us. And I was bound to that promise.

I shuddered at the thought that somewhere deep in my veins there was that magically sealed deal coursing in my human blood.

One of Queen Velraxis's guards rounded the corner, interrupting my thoughts. He clutched the reins which were attached to the most beautiful horse I had ever seen. This was clearly no normal horse. Its movements were unnaturally graceful, flowing like a stream of water, and its sleek black body was flecked with silver spots, as though the stars from the night sky had rained down upon its back and left their mark.

'We are providing you with a horse for the journey, else you will never get back in time. If you make it at all,' the guard sniped with a smirk. 'This is

Lumen. She will serve you for your journey.'

I ignored the comment he had made and approached her warily. She was magnetising and I reached out a hand to stroke her long nose; my hand met the softest velvety coat. She studied me with intelligent eyes, wide and hypnotic, like looking into a never-ending universe that transported you far, far, far away-

'Don't tell me you expect us to share the horse?' Sylas's voice sighed from under the helmet. The Fae guard fixed him with a glare.

I whirled around to him, squaring my shoulders. 'Listen, *buddy*, I'm not exactly thrilled about sharing this beautiful horse with you, but I guess we are stuck with one another for a whole month. So let's just get on with this. The quicker we do, the quicker we get back.'

Sylas didn't retort, but I could feel his surprise at my sharp response. The Fae guard glanced between us, and deciding I was the one in charge, handed me a pack that had been sitting on his shoulder.

'We are giving you this pack filled with the bare essentials, a bit of food, and some helpful tools so that you don't waste time faffing around. It won't last you the whole journey so be wise with it.'

I couldn't help but marvel at the pack: it was crafted from thick leaves, woven together by a thin white thread I assumed was spider silk, and the inside was lined with furry moss to keep our supplies warm and dry. I peeked into the many pockets: a compass, a hollowed gourd that served as a water bottle, a large chunk of bread, and some flint for starting fires. I still had some money in my cloak pocket left from when I had been abducted outside the tavern yesterday, so I dropped the coins inside. I knew humans lived in the Untamed Territory, scattered in villages, and could only pray they used the same currency as Nexonia, just in case we needed a place to sleep or, more importantly, a place to have a drink.

I swung the pack over my shoulders and looked at the guard expectantly. I wanted to get going now. Get away from the Fae, even if it meant heading into dangerous Untamed Territory.

'You will need to head that way, north,' the guard said as he jerked his chin into the shadowy depths beyond. 'It heads straight out of our land,

and once you leave the forest, you'll be in the Untamed Territory. Well, that's *if* you make it that far.' His mouth was a thin-lipped grimace. I could practically hear my dagger begging me to lodge it in the Fae's throat but thought better of it, and instead busied myself with the terrifying task of mounting Lumen, who towered above me. I managed to stick my foot into the stirrup and then pushed up on my heel, hauling myself up and grabbing onto the saddle. Feeling a little flustered but pleased with my success, I turned to Sylas impatiently.

'Come on, hurry up. Every second counts.'

His shoulders heaved a sigh, and he hauled himself up behind me with much more ease. We both shifted awkwardly in the saddle, trying to avoid touching each other - an almost impossible task. I had worried about the weight of two riders on Lumen's back, but she didn't seem bothered in the slightest. I didn't have anything more to say to the cruel Fae guard, so with that I clicked Lumen on, and we started on our journey to save the Heir, my parents, and Nexonia.

'Watch your back,' crooned the Fae, waving his spidery fingers at our retreating form.

Chapter Five

Lumen's long strides padded softly against the forest floor, the only sound in the silent night. The air had grown steadily colder as we moved through the trees, and I was very thankful for the thick cloak wrapped around me. Tilting my head up, I caught a glimpse of the inky sky and watched as the moons began to slide apart - becoming two separate orbs once again. The hour was up, and the Veil wouldn't be back down until next month. We had to time this journey perfectly.

Sylas and I hadn't exchanged a word since leaving the Faeries, which I didn't mind. I appreciated the silence with my head so full of gut-churning thoughts. Would we make it back in time for the next Night of Two Moons? Would we succeed? Would we even survive? Would my parent's death be quick if I failed, or would the Queen of Nexonia torture and punish them for my failures? I wondered if Sylas had a family who would miss him if we didn't make it. I didn't ask.

We rode on into the small hours of the morning. The adrenaline from the past few hours was still coursing through my veins, making me feel as though I could ride for days on end without stopping. But a more practical side of me knew better. This pace wasn't sustainable for a whole month, Lumen would need to graze, and we would all need to rest to stay sharp if we were to survive what lay ahead. We were heading into dangerous, unfamiliar territory, and exhaustion would only make us more vulnerable. Though fewer tales were whispered about the creatures of the Untamed Territory compared to the Fae, the rumours that did circulate were unsettling enough.

'Let's find a place to sleep for a few hours until dawn,' I said to Sylas, not bothering to look back as I spoke. He grunted, which I took as a yes. As we continued, I scanned the surroundings for a somewhat comfortable-looking place to set up camp. Eventually, my eyes snagged a thick tree with three forking branches. Where they intersected, a small nook was formed, just large enough that I would be able to tuck myself into it, and the base of the tree was padded with a thick layer of springy moss which would be the perfect resting spot for Sylas. I guided Lumen toward it, and the moment we stopped moving, Sylas swung off her back with ease.

For me, it was a bit more of a challenge. Lumen stood taller than any normal horse, and I bit my lip as I studied the ground looming far below.

'Do you need some help?' Sylas asked flatly; his head cocked to one side.

'No, I'm good,' I muttered. Then more to myself than Sylas, 'I got this.'

I didn't.

To my horror, he stood and watched as I then leaned forward and swung a leg over Lumen's body, slowly lowering myself as near to the forest floor as possible before dropping the rest of the way. I stumbled as I hit the ground and found myself flying backward. Strong hands caught me before I could crash into the earth. Sylas righted me before I could brush his arms off.

'Thanks,' I coughed.

Sylas said nothing but slumped against the tree, resting his forearms on his knees, and so I settled myself opposite as I opened up the pack and extracted the bread we had been gifted. I gave it a sniff. I wasn't sure if I wanted to eat it. I certainly didn't trust the Faeries one bit.

'They wouldn't poison it,' Sylas sighed, his eyes unlocatable behind the helmet. 'They wouldn't have bothered sending us on this journey and given us supplies if they planned on killing us with bread.'

I stopped sniffing it and offered him my middle finger. I suppose it was true though. I ripped off two chunks and handed Sylas one before tucking the rest of the bread away. When I turned back, Sylas was studying his portion.

'You're going to actually have to take your helmet off if you want to eat that,' I said slowly, as if he were thick. He paused for a few beats but then reached up, yanking the helmet off his head.

I choked on my saliva.

That was not the kind of face that belonged under a helmet. He pushed back a few dark curls from his eyes - his *eyes*. They were unlike anything I had ever seen. One was as deep and brown as tree bark, while the other shone green, vivid as sunlight through spring leaves. Those eyes caught mine as I stared, and I blinked quickly, looking down at the bread still clutched in my hands. I took a bite, forgetting to be cautious, and my eyes widened at the taste.

I thought it had just been a chunk of plain bread, but it tasted incredible, tingling in my mouth with sweet notes of honey, dark cherry, and vanilla. I savoured it before regretfully swallowing, and the minute I did I felt a tightening sensation in my stomach, as if it had just shrunk to the size of a prune. Only moments ago I had been starving, but after that tiny bite, I felt as though I had eaten a full-course meal. I stared in awe at the remaining chunk left in my hand.

'It's Fae bread, what did you expect?' Sylas mused, his voice clearer and filled with boyish cockiness now that the helmet had been removed. I let my face drop of all reaction. He might be handsome, but he was a pain in the ass. Sylas took a bite of his own bread and handed the excess back to me, dusting his hands off before he began to walk off.

'Erm, where do you think you're going?' I shouted after him.

He didn't bother turning back to face me as he said, 'To get some dry wood for a fire. You should get some sleep, you're very grouchy. I won't be long.'

I uttered an incredulous gasp. Everyone was testing my patience today.

'What about Lumen? Don't we need to tie her up or something?' I said, getting to my feet.

Sylas was still walking away, his voice fading as he said 'No, she won't go anywhere. Fae horses are no doubt smart, and she's been assigned to stay with us so she won't go anywhere.'

And off he went, disappearing into the night. Anger curled inside my stomach. I extracted my dagger, hurling it with precision at a tree just east of where Sylas had stood seconds ago. It thudded into the bark with a satisfying crunch. I breathed out slowly. How would I put up with this man for a whole month? I extracted the dagger from the bark and allowed myself to launch my dagger at some more trees until my anger loosened its hold on me.

Eventually I clambered into the nook of the tree, using the pack as my pillow and my cloak as a blanket. It wasn't too uncomfy, the moss carpeted me from underneath, and when I tucked my legs in, I was a perfect fit. My eyes grew heavy quickly, I was exhausted from the stress of the day. At some point, I drifted off to sleep, dreaming a terrible dream where the Queen of Nexonia was torturing my parents in front of me for having failed my mission.

Chapter Six

Buttery fingers of sunlight streaming through the canopy awoke me. For a moment I'm dazed, my brain scrabbling to understand why I'm in a forest and why my muscles feel so stiff. Then it all came flooding back. One terrible memory crashing into another.

I sat upright, twisting my body this way and that to loosen the tension seizing up my muscles. Sylas was down below, his back to me as he settled against the tree, a burnt-out fire before him. He must have made it while I slept. I dropped out from my sleeping nook, stretching my joints and hearing them crack in complaint after having squished myself up all night.

My heart dropped suddenly as I remembered Lumen - where was she? I spun on the spot, breathing a sigh of relief as I spotted her intensely sniffing the ground a short distance away. I watched with curiosity as she kept walking along, her muzzle pressed firmly to the ground as she rummaged around twigs and leaves. It was like she was sniffing out a trail. Her nose located a small hole, and with a sudden motion she began to dig her nose into the ground, shifting the loose soil to the side. She dove into the hole with her teeth, extracting something small and fuzzy - a mole.

With one fluid motion, Lumen tipped her head back and the mole went flying into the air before she caught it swiftly. Bones crunched as she chewed happily, her long tail swishing.

'What in the Veil,' I gasped.

'You didn't truly expect a Fae horse like that to eat grass like a normal one, did you?' Sylas's voice came from behind, making me jump. He watched me with an eyebrow raised, but a glimmer of amusement twinkled somewhere deep within those fascinating eyes.

I drew my eyebrows together, 'No, course not. I always see carnivorous horses back in Nexonia, munching on moles and such, so this comes as no surprise,' I retorted. So they had bread that filled you up with a single bite, and horses that ate meat - I guess I shouldn't be shocked at any more of these surprises along the way.

Sylas just shook his head gently. He looked tired, purple crescents sat under his eyes, giving him a handsomely haunted look. I felt a twinge of guilt for having given myself the better sleeping position. Perhaps if we made it to the Untamed tonight, we could find a village to stay in so he could have a proper rest.

We had a small chunk of bread for our breakfast and a drink from the gourd before mounting Lumen, who was still swishing her tail contently. She trotted merrily along the packed dirt as we rode. Thick ferns grew on either side of us, brushing my ankles, while dappled sunlight cast patterns of light dancing through the trees. I had never seen so much greenery. It was so... quiet here. So peaceful. Nothing like the constant rumble of noise in Nexonia; hearing people's rows through thin walls, horses' hooves clomping along the cobblestone at midnight, drunkards yelling in the street, laughter and gossiping. I missed my parents' laughter, that delightful sound that lit up my heart and made me forget who I was for a moment. Forget that I was a killer.

As we continued, I heard a distant hushing sound. I held my breath, my heart pumping a bit faster. It sounded like... a stream. I gave Lumen a small squeeze to the sides and she trotted into a clearing, and there it was, babbling away. Sunlight made the water sparkle as it tinkered over mossy rocks, carving its way through the forest floor.

I swung my leg over Lumen, ready to slide down, when Sylas put a hand on my arm.

'Woah, what are you doing?'

I wrinkled my forehead. 'I just want to wash my face quickly, I feel grubby. I won't be a moment.'

Sylas shook his head, 'We don't have time. We need to keep moving.'

I gave his fingers on my arm a painful flick and he removed his hand. I slid down from Lumen and thankfully landed on my feet this time. 'Listen, if you want to be smelly and gross, then that's your business. It will take one minute at best.' I backed towards the stream as he rolled his eyes. As I turned away, I grumbled, 'Keep your pants on, you grump.'

Kneeling by the stream I eased the pack off my back, scooping my hands into the cool water and bringing it up to my face to scrub off the dirt and moss staining my cheeks. I cupped my hands and took another scoop, tipping the water down my throat.

Much better.

As I straightened up, feeling refreshed, a sudden loud buzzing erupted near my ear. I swatted at the insect without thinking, only to freeze in horror when it let out a sharp, high-pitched screech. I stumbled backwards, falling on my rear. That's when I saw it clearly - I screamed. A small, mean blue face with wide eyes screeched back at me. Its tiny body was held aloft by four rapidly beating wings, and its hands ended in three sharp, claw-like fingers. A pixie.

'What's wrong?' Sylas shouted from Lumen's back. No doubt he was unable to see the tiny creature from the distance between us. Before I could open my mouth to reply, the buzzing turned into a swarm. The air came alive as ten more blue bodies joined their friend, and they were all upon me - pulling my hair, tugging my ears, climbing into my cloak. I writhed and called out, slapping different parts of my body and swatting my hand in the air.

Through the chaos, I could now see another group of pixies were attacking Sylas and Lumen now. They were crawling through Lumen's beautiful mane, ripping out chunks, and swarming around Sylas's head.

I didn't know what to do - they were relentless. There was no use drawing my dagger against them, they were much too nimble to be struck by the tiny blade and they would most likely snatch it from my fingers and use it against me. These pixies were one of the few creatures I had heard from Nexonia's tales, and from what I knew, they loved nothing more than causing mischief and chaos.

I got to my feet and ran blindly, but wherever I went, they followed. I could feel them crawling about in my hair. We were outnumbered by far. Wicked chuckles filled the air. They were having fun, and tormenting us was their entertainment. I had to do something now; they could keep this up for hours and we didn't have time to waste.

I flipped my head upside down, raking my fingers through my hair to dislodge the pixies. I caught sight of a large stick through the tangled strands that knotted in front of my face. I sprinted for it, picked it up, and whirled around, ready for the pixies to follow. As the first one flew at me, I took aim. My precision was unmatched, thanks to many years of intensive target practice, and the stick connected with the pixie's body, sending it sprawling. It smashed against a tree and slid down the length of it to the forest floor, groaning. I turned back to the others, who had come zooming my way but now halted mid-air, staring in awe at their unconscious friend. The grins dropped from their little faces.

I beckoned them like a mad-woman, my hair messed up and my eyes crazed, yielding the stick in my hands. If anything was going to prevent me from getting this Divinal Stone, I would not let it be these stupid pixies. They gazed at me, lips trembling now that I had just spoiled their fun.

'Come on then,' I beckoned again. 'Who wants to go next?'

The pixie at the very front of the swarm let out a whimper before turning and racing away. The others all followed suit, whistling to the group harassing Lumen and Sylas, who promptly left them alone to fly off with the rest of the herd. I let out a breath, dropping the stick, my hands on my knees as I panted.

'Is everyone alright?' I said, coming to check on Lumen and Sylas. Chunks of Lumen's mane were gone, but other than that she was untouched. Sylas, on the other hand, looked thoroughly ruffled. His hair stuck up at odd angles, his cloak had been pulled halfway off his shoulders. Although I felt awful for having been the reason we got ambushed, I bit the inside of my cheek to stifle the laughter bubbling within.

'Yeah, we are great. Thanks, Aurora,' he huffed.

I let my jaw drop, 'How was I supposed to know that would happen?'

'I told you we shouldn't have stopped. But no, Princess Aurora needed to wash her face and look perfect, even though we are on a *mission*, not going to a fancy ball.'

I opened my mouth to retort when I was struck with a thought. I turned back to the stream and my heart plummeted.

'Where's the pack?'

It was gone. I had taken it off by the river and now it was gone. Sylas groaned into his hands. He dismounted and we both searched everywhere for it; in the ferns, along the stream, inside a hollowed-out log. It was nowhere to be seen. Sylas dragged a hand through his hair.

Behind me Lumen whinnied and jerked her head upwards. I followed her gaze before letting out a string of curses. There was the pack, sitting on the uppermost branch of a tall tree, its strap looped around a thin limb near the top. Sylas stood next to me, hands on his hips.

'Well, that's fantastic. What are we going to do now?'

I studied the tree. I hadn't climbed one since I was young, but I had practised scaling buildings as part of my assassin's training - how different could it be? But I knew already that the upmost branches were going to be a problem as they were much too thin to bear my weight. I blew out air from my mouth, trying to think. We needed that pack badly, there was no way we could leave without it. My heart pummelled against my chest, a countdown for every second we were wasting.

Something warm nudged my arm. I turned to find Lumen trying to get my attention. She held something between her teeth, so I held out my hand and she gently dropped the now-semi-conscious pixie into it.

That was it. That was my solution.

'Good thinking, girl!' I nodded to Lumen, bending down to unlace my boot. I pulled the long string out, tying it to the pixie's waist and straightened out its tiny wings, which were bent at an angle from the force of hitting the tree. It must have hurt a great deal, as the pixie gasped awake, blinking in the sunlight. I tightened my grip on it and brought it close to my face.

'You and your little friends thought it would be funny to put our pack up

40

there,' I pointed to where the pack dangled far above. 'And now you're going to get it down for me. And if you fail, my companion here likes to *eat* little disobedient pixies.'

I held the pixie up to Lumen, who seemed to comprehend the threat I was making, and snapped her teeth inches from the pixie's face. I highly doubted the creature could understand what I was saying, so for good measure I prodded it in the chest then indicated to my pack. It looked at the pack in the branches, and then to me, before blowing a raspberry right in my face.

I kept the pixie clutched tightly in my fist as I began to climb the tree, as high as my weight would allow me. Sylas watched with his arms crossed from down below.

'Don't fall,' he said unhelpfully.

'Great advice,' I said through gritted teeth, 'Not sure what I would do without you.'

Climbing the tree was hard work, made even harder by the fact I could only grip with one hand. But I was determined. Determined that this setback would not prevent us from getting that Stone. I reached the highest point I could go, from here the branches were too thin and spindly to bare me, they would snap as soon as I used them to haul myself up any further. The pack was just above, so near but just about out of my reach.

I made the mistake of looking down. The ground loomed far below, Sylas and Lumen like miniature figures. One slip and I was done for. The pixie must have noticed the flicker of worry possess my face because it snickered nastily. I held it close to my face and whispered, 'Let's hope your wings aren't too damaged then, it's a long drop.'

I threw its body towards the pack, holding onto the lace I had attached around it like a leash. The pixie dropped for a moment, caught off-guard, before catching itself and hovering mid-air. It stayed there, giving me an angry stare, so I gave the shoe-lace leash a tug. I was blown another raspberry before it reluctantly flew over to the pack.

'Try and slide it off the branch,' I urged, miming pushing an imaginary pack in hopes that the pixie would copy. The creature rolled its eyes but started to shove the pack anyway. It slid closer and closer to the edge of the branch, which began to sag as the weight shifted along. The pixie was struggling, its tiny body only able to push it bit by bit, but eventually, the pack was hanging right on the edge.

'Good, now bring it to me,' I urged, holding out a hand towards it. The pixie began jabbering away in a foreign, high voice, shaking its fist at me before booting the pack with all its might. The pack flung off the branch and plummeted to the ground. I cringed, watching it fall. But Sylas was ready down below, he caught it neatly before it could smash against the ground. I released the breath I was holding. Thank the Veil.

'That will do,' I sighed, before yanking the pixie towards me. I clasped it tightly in my fist again before I clambered back down the tree, not daring to untie it until my feet had safely reached the ground.

'Go find your little pals who ditched you,' I said, finally throwing it into the air.

The minute it was free the pixie zoomed into the air, not before making a gesture to me I could only assume was very rude in their language.

Sarcasm dripped from my every word as I called after it, 'Sorry for smashing you around the face!'

Sylas's mouth twitched but he shook his head at me. 'Alright, let's get moving. We have wasted enough time today.'

We decided to ride on that day and skip lunch to make up for the time lost. Lumen took off at a sprint, and it wasn't long until the wind was screaming in my ears, my thick red hair now bound in a plait, thumping against my shoulder with every stride.

Little did we know, this was only the first of many challenges we would face.

Chapter Seven

As darkness fell behind us my stomach began to growl. I was starving, my stomach felt like an empty, churning pit. Lumen had now slowed to a walking pace to preserve her energy. I expected we would be reaching the end of the Fae Land soon, seeing as we had headed in a straight line for a good few miles now.

I decided to check the compass to ensure we were staying on track to head north. I rummaged through the numerous pack pockets and pulled it out. My brows knitted together in confusion as I beheld the compass.

It was matte black, with fine golden details, and while it had a needle indicating we were indeed headed north, there was also a second needle that twitched wildly. It would point north for a moment, then swivel back to point south - the way we had just come - before swinging back to north again. I held the compass up for Sylas to see.

'Look at this. It has *two* needles. What do you think the second one is for?'

He took it from me and studied it carefully before shrugging. 'Maybe it's broken. The first needle shows we're heading north, so that one is correct. We'll keep following that.'

I took the compass back from him, unconvinced. Even if it was broken, why was there a second needle in the first place when there was already one that worked?

I tucked it back into the pack beside the bread, the sight of which made my stomach growl again. Although I was starving, I was keen to ration the bread as much as possible as we had a long way to go. It was quiet for some time, until another growl shattered the silence.

'Veil above, just eat some bread,' Sylas sighed, exasperated.

Unease turned my blood cold. 'That wasn't my stomach this time, Sylas,' I said slowly. Another growl sounded out, this time it was clearer, coming from the tangle of ferns beside us.

'Shit,' Sylas muttered. It was then that I felt a presence beside us, stalking along the other side of the ferns. Lumen seemed to sense it too, for she tossed her head about. I leant forward, stroking her back and hushing her. Something was following us.

'Easy, girl. Easy, hush now,' I said, patting her neck. I was trying to soothe her but my own heart was hammering in my throat. I leant back and whispered, 'Sylas, what do we do?'

On either side of us, I could see dark shapes lurking behind the gaps in the leaves. Somewhere up ahead there was a howl, a deep and stomach-churning sound. We were being surrounded, and they were closing in. A strong metallic tang floated in the breeze. I could taste the salty freshness on my tongue. Blood.

Without warning, a black blur streaked toward us from the left, crashing through the ferns. The hound's white fangs gleamed under the moonlight, its eyes wild and crazed.

'Go!' Sylas shouted. Lumen didn't need to be told twice. She broke into a gallop, her hooves thundering against the forest floor. The trees around us blurred into dark smudges as we tore ahead. I could hear the hound's heavy breaths behind us, only a few feet away. Slowly, a faint light appeared in the distance, growing stronger with each stride. My heart leapt at the sight of an opening - the end of the forest.

Pinpricks of light flickered just beyond. A village.

Salvation.

But the snarls of our pursuers echoed through the trees, closer with each second. I dared a glance over my shoulder, and my blood ran cold. More hounds were emerging from the shadows, six huge, midnight-black hounds, their mouths foaming, eyes locked on us. Their growls rippled through the night air.

I dug my heels deeper into Lumen's sides, urging her to keep going. She was as fast as anything, but after a long day of travel with no rest, she was running on borrowed strength. Pure adrenaline drove her now, but I knew it wouldn't last.

'Come on, girl! Faster, Lumen!' I pleaded. The hounds were so close now, their jaws snapped at Lumen's hind legs. She whinnied in terror, her hooves pounding harder against the earth. We were so close to reaching the end of the forest, the village so near... but then a hulking shape stepped out ahead, blocking our clear path.

A hound positioned himself directly in our way, his snarls tearing through the air as it watched us get closer and closer with hungry eyes. There was nowhere else to turn. They were closing in from every direction. I gave Lumen a sharp kick, urging her not to slow. As we barrelled forward, I bent low, fumbling for the dagger wedged in my boot. I wobbled a little, almost toppling off as Lumen jumped over a fallen log and immediately Sylas's hands were on my waist to steady me.

I managed to right myself, the blood beating in my ears. The hound ahead barked, muscles tensing as it prepared to lunge. To take us down and eat us alive. Behind us, the pack closed in, their breaths haggard. This was it.

I had one chance.

I focused on the lead hound blocking our path, closing one eye as I took my aim. Time seemed to slow as I raised the dagger, its weight solid in my grip, and I let the world fall away. Everything narrowed down to my target.

With practised aim I let the dagger fly, it overtook us, the blade winking as it rotated under the moonlight, and found its way straight into the hound's heart. It yelped, staggering over its own legs before collapsing, leaving our path open once more.

'Don't let go,' I shouted to Sylas, feeling his grip tighten on my waist as I leaned dangerously low off Lumen's side. The forest was thinning, and the village lights were clear up ahead. I bent lower, my body practically hanging off the saddle now as we surged forward. I waited for the perfect moment before snatching my dagger from the dead hound's chest, sending a spray of blood straight into my face. I gasped, blinking rapidly to clear my vision, and when I re-opened my eyes there was a hound's face inches from my own, its jaws open wide to rip my face off.

Before I could even scream, Sylas had hoisted me up again, and we broke through the line of trees, out into the open. Lumen didn't stop as she stormed towards the village. Looking back, I saw the hounds had stopped where the trees did, growling viciously after us but then they turned reluctantly and headed back into the dark depths of the Fae Land. We had made it. To the Untamed Territory.

We approached the village, all of us panting heavily, bodies still coursing with adrenaline. No one spoke, but I didn't need to ask to know we were all thinking the same thing - this village would be our refuge for the night. Lumen's flanks heaved with exhaustion, her breaths coming in short, laboured gasps. She had pushed herself to the limit today, and it was clear she needed rest. We all did.

I slid off her back, my legs shaking but steady enough to land without collapsing. Sylas dismounted too; his eyes wide.

'That thing you did with the dagger,' Sylas said between heavy breaths, 'was *insane*. You could kill for a living.'

I huffed a laugh at his sarcasm and did a little curtsey. I felt light-headed after our near-death experience and was excited with the prospect of sleeping the night in a real bed. I would have taken a thousand pixies over those hounds.

'Right, let's get some rest, if possible,' I said, leading Lumen by the reins to the towering iron gates ahead.

But Sylas touched me lightly on the arm. 'You might want to scrub the blood from your face first. I'm not sure they will let you in if you look like a murdering savage.' He tugged down the hem of his shirt and tore away a strip of fabric, handing it to me. 'You can use this, it's clean.'

I thanked him and rubbed at my face with the material he handed me. It came back stained with dark blood, still warm from the hound. I glanced at Sylas, seeking his approval, and he gave a quick nod. I turned my gaze back to the village gates ahead.

They were tall and spiked, which made sense in order to keep out creatures like the hounds that had nearly torn us apart. Unlike Nexonia - the part of these lands under our Queen's rule - the people in the Untamed Territory were unprotected. They had their own ways of defending themselves against the lurking dangers beyond. The people here were descendants of an older generation from Nexonia, those who had left to seek the freedom of life beyond any King or Queen's rule, choosing the dangers of the Untamed over submission. Now, most of those original settlers were gone, and their offspring, born into the Territory, knew no other life. Yet they carried on their ancestors' spirit of fierce independence.

As we approached, we found a hardy man patrolling behind the gates, a well-worn spear gripped in his hands. His gaze swept over us, travelling over me, then Sylas, and then to Lumen. I had already stuffed my dagger into my cloak pocket, the hound blood still fresh on the blade. I wanted us to look as less intimidating as possible.

Up close, the man's skin looked rough and weathered, like old leather left out in the sun too long. It was peppered with pink scars that stood out against the darker skin, no doubt caused by battles with hounds and other creatures of the Untamed Territory.

'You both look a right state, don't ya? Where've you come from?' His was voice was not unkind, but it was firm. The kind of firmness that told me he dealt with no nonsense, and we would not be allowed access to the village unless we answered his questions correctly.

In these parts, everyone was for themselves, and strangers were most likely not a common sight, so trust was not given freely. We most definitely couldn't say we were from the other side of the Veil, from the land ruled by the Queen of Nexonia. Mentioning any connection to the Queen now would only make us enemies.

Despite the wave of exhaustion that had begun to drain me of energy, I fixed the man with a beaming smile that hopefully showed we were friend, not foe. 'We come from a village just east from here. We were just travelling along when those hounds came for us - out of nowhere - catching us off guard. We are just looking for a place to stay for the night to catch our breath.'

I gestured between us, trying to seem as casual as possible. Sylas attempted a smile, though it came out more like a grimace. My smile dropped as I beheld Lumen. She looked completely different. She had glamoured herself to appear more like an ordinary horse - something I hadn't even thought to worry about. She must have realised that if she remained in her true Fae form, we might have been cast out on sight. Yet even in this disguise, she was still striking, her coat a sleek black flecked with shimmering white.

The man was nodding at her approvingly, 'Beautiful horsie. Yeah, would have been a right shame if she got eaten by those bloody things. Alright, come on in, but watch your step. People are always wary of outsiders around here.' He turned his back to us and pulled on a lever, cranking the gate open just wide enough for us to fit through. We slipped through the gap, and I made sure to give him another reassuring smile as I went.

'Usually there is a room or two available at the tavern, but you might be out of luck tonight as we had some traders come to stay today. Your best bet might be knocking on a few doors, some of em' might let you stay if you give em' a penny or two,' the man advised.

We made our way through the village, which was sturdy as old boots, with thick iron shutters on houses, bunches of rosemary tied with red string were nailed onto doors, watchmen patrolled with iron-tipped spears, their faces hard and set. All the security measures should have made me feel panicked that it was necessary at all, but instead it made me feel safe. I was glad we were inside the walls rather than having to face what was out there for the night. It seemed the people here were always ready, prepared for the worst. They looked after themselves and protected their village.

At the end of the row of houses, I spotted a stone building with a metal sign attached, flapping in the breeze; The Green Man. Out the front of the tavern was a small stable area that had two spaces to hold horses.

'I'm going to grab a drink, Veil knows I need it,' I said, jerking a thumb at the tavern. 'I'll ask at the bar if we can keep Lumen in there for the night.' I turned to make my way over, before stopping in my tracks. Sylas had saved me from having my face chewed off by that hound, I needed to be polite. Digging my fingernails into my palms, I added, 'Care to join?'

To my relief he shook his head, sending curls skittering across his forehead.

He ran a hand through them. 'I need some rest so I better start knocking on doors to see if someone will let me stay for the night. Have a drink on me.' He dug out a coin from his pocket and flicked it with a thumb at me. I snatched it as it flew across the air. As I turned again, he called out 'Try not to be ambushed by any more pixies or hounds.'

I exhaled. 'I can't promise that.'

I led Lumen into one of the small stables, stroking her muzzle and whispering my apologies. She was so intelligent that it felt like an insult to put her in this dingy old stable, but short of bringing her into the tavern with me, there was nothing else I could do. She eyed the bundle of soggy hay with disdain.

'Don't worry girl, I'll bring some fresh meat for you if I can, okay?' I gave her one last apologetic nuzzle.

The minute I stepped into the tavern, I was hit with two sensations; firstly, how toasty it was, and the second was the noise. I shed my cloak, folding it over the pack bundled in my arms and made my way toward the bar at the other end. Large black beams stretched overhead, oil lamps flickered on the many tables crammed against walls, lighting up people's faces with an excited, merry glow. From one of the tables near the fire, a group of drinkers had broken into a tuneless song, their faces flushed red with drink as they swayed. It was the kind of place where, for a moment, you could forget the dangers that lurked outside.

Nobody glanced my way, perhaps they weren't bothered with newcomers, which worked well for me. I slid into a stool at the bar, tapping Sylas's coin gently on the wooden countertop as I drunk in the lively scenes.

'I haven't seen you before,' the bartender said. He had a face like a basset hound, lined with many wrinkles, and a great hooked nose that probably proceeded the entrance to rooms before he did.

'I'm not from here. Spiced ale, please,' I said, rubbing my temples. I felt a raging headache coming on. 'And do you know anywhere I can stay the night?'

The man shook his head as he poured amber liquid into a grubby glass.

'Nah, my rooms here are full, not that I have many. You will have to ask around.'

As soon as the drink was set in front of me, I knocked it back, the burn of the liquor warming my throat. I slid Sylas's coin across the counter cautiously, my eyes flicking to the barkeep's face. I watched closely for any sign that he didn't recognise the currency - wondering if, over here, they might have developed a different form of payment since leaving Nexonia.

But the bartender didn't say a word as he swept the coin into his hand and tucked it in his pocket, refilling my glass too. I scanned the room again, the people here seemed lively, but I didn't know how I felt about asking to stay with one of them. I wondered if Sylas had had any success. Perhaps I could share the stable with Lumen, maybe if I found some fresh hay, I could fashion some kind of a bed-

'I have a spare room, love,' a voice like soft chimes floated from the other side of the bar. 'It's my daughter's. It's only small, mind, but she's away for the next few weeks, so it's available if you want it.'

I grabbed my glass and rounded the bar to see my saviour. A small woman sat on a stool, her legs dangling as they didn't quite reach the floor. She looked even older than the bartender, with grey hair neatly tucked into a bun at the back of her head, soft tendrils escaping to frame her face. Normally I'd be wary if someone offered me a room so easily, but there was something about her that made me feel at ease. Her eyes, soft and crinkled at the corners, held a warmth that willed me to trust her.

'That is so kind of you. How much?' I said, undoing the clasps on the pack but she held up a hand.

'No money. The company is payment enough. I miss my daughter dreadfully and you remind me of her, with your gorgeous red hair. When you walked in the tavern, I thought it was her for a second.' She smiled at the braid sat on my shoulder. 'No, the room is free of charge.'

Other than my parents, my trust had been sealed off from others for years. There had been a time when I had loved and trusted someone else - once. But that trust had been shattered, scrunched up and thrown back in my face, leaving me wary of opening my heart to anyone other than my parents ever again. Since then, I had hardened myself, always keeping people at arm's

50

length. But here was this old woman, missing her daughter and wanting some company.

The anxiety that had been bubbling in my stomach at the thought of sleeping in the hay eased. 'That is so kind of you, truly. I didn't catch your name?'

'Patricia, love. But call me Pat. Take a seat, you look exhausted,' she patted a hand to the stool beside her. She was right, I *was* exhausted. 'Where have you come from?'

I told her the same lie I told the man guarding the gates and she nodded eagerly. 'Ah, just like my Jess. She travels from village to village selling goods and materials and doing trades. It means she's gone for months at a time, and I do worry about her. It's hard out there, but luckily she travels with a big group of others, which makes me feel better. Where are you heading to now?'

I opened my mouth to answer, before swiftly closing it again. I was stumped by the question. It was only then that I realised I wasn't quite sure. My goal for the past day had been to reach the end of the Fae Land and get to the Untamed, and now we were here… we needed to find the weapon that Queen Merida and the priest had created. But where to even begin?

'You don't know of any churches nearby, do you?' I asked Pat. I thought it would be most logical to look for the weapon there, since it was a priest who Merida had worked with to create it. I doubt he was alive anymore though, if these visions and conflicts had happened fifty years ago.

Pat shook her head, 'None that I know of, no. But there will be some about, perhaps further up north.'

I pulled the compass from my pack to get my bearings. If we continued forward, past this village, we would be heading north. The second needle was still twitching unhelpfully, torn whether it wanted to point north or south, the way we had just come. When Pat caught sight of the compass she gasped, quickly stifling it with a cough.

My heart plummeted. How could I have been so careless? This was clearly no ordinary compass, and I had just exposed it in front of someone who must have recognised its significance. My fingers trembled as I stuffed it back into my pack, my ears burning with embarrassment.

Pat leaned forward, placing a gentle hand on mine. In a low voice, she warned, 'Don't let anyone else see that, love. You might find yourself in trouble.'

Her deep, brown eyes were wide.

'You know what this is?' I whispered. Of course I knew she recognised it was a compass. What I was really asking was; *you know who this belongs to, don't you?*

Pat nodded. 'It's a Desire Compass.' She leaned in further until our foreheads were nearly touching. 'Where did you get this from?'

'I- I found it,' I lied. My palms felt slick. Her eyes scanned my face, and she nodded slowly.

'If you say so, love. But maybe it's best you keep it in your pack for now, until you leave the village.'

'You called it a Desire Compass?' I breathed. 'What does that mean?'

Pat's eyes flicked around the tavern, watching the faces of those lost in conversation or song. She shuffled her stool even closer. In a low, hushed tone, she whispered, 'As you've probably gathered by now, a Desire Compass is no ordinary compass. Yes, it has a needle that indicates north, but there's also a second needle. This one points toward whatever it is you desire most in that moment, even if you don't yet know what that is.'

My jaw dropped. It made complete sense. When Sylas and I had been heading north at the start of the journey, the desire needle had twitched madly, first pointing north and then south. It was because my desire was divided. Part of me wanted to keep heading north because the weapon we needed lay ahead, but another part of me wanted to turn around and go back to my parents.

So perhaps if I concentrated on my desire to find the weapon which would destroy the Shadow Warden, it would lead me there.

'How do you know this?' I found myself saying.

'I am *very* old and *very* wise, if I do say so myself,' Pat said, with a knowing smile. 'This village is close to the edge of the Fae Land here. They don't cross over much anymore, but they used to many years ago, slipping into the Untamed Territory for all sorts of reasons. Who knows what they were up to. And on rare occasions, they'd speak to us or accidently drop things. Over the years, we collected whatever we found - studying them, writing about them in books. It's always good to know all their tools and tricks. I've read about a Desire Compass before... but never have I actually seen one.' She shook her head, leaning back. 'It's best not to discuss here.'

We moved on to talking about other things, which I was grateful for: her life in the village, her daughter. She tactfully didn't ask me any more questions about myself. I ordered some food too: a hearty stew, full of mutton that melted in the mouth, and potatoes and carrots. I drank it up quickly, savouring the warm liquid flowing down my throat. I relished the taste. Whilst the Faery bread was delicious, it was nice to feel normal and sit down and have a proper meal again.

When no one was watching, I quietly wrapped a few pieces of mutton in a napkin and slipped it into my pocket. After finishing my meal, we left the tavern, but I told Pat I wanted to check on my horse quickly. She waited while I said goodnight to Lumen, and when Pat's back was turned, I pulled the mutton from my pocket and fed it to her. She nuzzled me appreciatively.

'I'll be back for you in the morning, girl,' I promised.

Pat's home, like the others in the village, had a modest, plain exterior. The walls were uneven, made of rough, grey stone that looked as though it had stood for centuries, and the roof was made from thatched straw. Her door was splintered but sturdy, with a round chalk symbol drawn onto it.

But the inside was another world.

We entered into a living room which already had a roaring fire going, filling the air with a smoky haze. Almost every surface was crammed with trinkets and charms of some kind; glass spheres, carved wooden amulets hung on the walls, bowls of salt, small wooden figurines. I observed them all with interest, trying to work out what the purpose for each object might be, but soon my attention waned as exhaustion overrode anything else.

I was hardly aware of Pat, who was nattering on about something that I hadn't been listening to. She laughed softly.

'Apologies, my dear. I've been talking your ear off, haven't I? I've been so lonely for so long that I sometimes catch myself chatting to nobody at all. Now that I finally have some company, I'm beside myself!' she chuckled, clutching my arm. 'Let's get you some rest.'

I went to protest but a yawn rudely interrupted, so I let her guide me through the narrow hallways. She shuffled along and pushed open a door at the end, revealing a snug little room that seemed to wrap itself around you like a warm embrace. An iron-wrought bed nestled against the walls, above which hung a threaded dreamcatcher, there was also a little nightstand and matching wooden wardrobe. Despite the fact Pat said her daughter hadn't been home in weeks, there wasn't a speck of dust or hint of a cobweb - a sure sign Pat missed her daughter dearly and looked after her room whilst she was gone.

'There is a chamber pot under the bed. You can borrow Jess's nightwear, she won't mind. If you need anything else, just shout, I will only be at the other end of the hall,' Pat said, closing the door with a smile on her face. As soon as the door clicked shut, I kicked off my boots and stripped my clothes off. I grabbed a random nightdress from the draw and slipped it over my head before collapsing onto the sheets. It spent the last of my energy.

I sank into a sleep so deep that even the nightmares couldn't reach me.

Chapter Eight

I was treated to a hearty breakfast the next morning; a sugary porridge drizzled generously with honey. Despite my objections, Pat insisted on packing some food for my journey. She claimed it was no trouble at all, saying she had prepared some food yesterday anyway and wanted me to take it before it spoiled. I knew this wasn't true, given the fresh smell of cooked beef that filled the air when I woke up. Since I mentioned I was travelling with a friend, she had prepared extra: two beef and cheese sandwiches for each of us, a couple of oatcakes, some nuts to share, and a few crisp apples.

At the threshold of her house, I found myself wrapping her into a hug. She was the first person other than my parents to show me such kindness in a long time. When I withdrew from the hug, I gathered her soft, wrinkled hands.

'Thank you, for everything. You are so kind. Your daughter is a lucky girl to have you.'

Pat's eyes grew watery. 'And thank *you* for putting up with a lonely widows rambling. Be safe love, remember, the further north you head, the more dangerous it gets. Keep your wits about you, be careful who you trust, avoid large bodies of water if you can.' Despite being in her house still, she dropped her voice to a whisper, as though the walls themselves could hear secrets. 'Only use that compass when you and your companion are *alone*.' She squeezed my fingers and gave a firm nod of the head.

I didn't want to leave her as she wrapped me up in one final hug. But I had to get the Divinal Stone. I had to save my parents.

So that is what I would do.

I squinted in the early morning sunshine. The air was ripe, crisp. As I approached Lumen's stable, I found Sylas leaning up against the wall, his head tilted back as he soaked in the weak sunlight. He looked down as I approached, and I could tell instantly that a proper night's sleep had done him good. The shadows under his eyes had dissipated and there was a healthy glow about his face.

'Where did you stay last night?'

He drew his eyebrows together. 'Good morning to you too, Aurora.'

'Where?' I repeated, curious.

Sylas tilted his head. 'Wouldn't you like to know, Princess?'

'Yeah, I would, that's why I asked.' I said, crossing my arms. 'And drop the Princess. I'm anything but.'

Just then some girls from the village walked by, they caught sight of Sylas and began whispering amongst themselves, giggling and throwing looks his way. I turned back to Sylas with disgust written over my face.

'Oh, Veil above, you didn't-'

Sylas's smirk dropped instantly when he realised what I was insinuating. 'No- no! Absolutely not. I was just messing with you,' he said quickly. 'The truth is I ended up staying at some man's house, he absolutely reeked. I didn't see a single bar of soap or basin in his house. He just tossed me some blankets and I ended up sleeping on the floor.'

I shook my head at him, tutting. 'Anyway, enough of this talk. Let's head onwards. I think I know where we need to head now, but,' I stole a glance around us to check nobody was nearby. 'I have some information about the compass to tell you once we are out of here.'

Sylas gave me a tight-lipped nod. As we rode back through the gates, the hardy man tipped his cap and wished us well on our journey. I felt a small wave of sadness wash over me, already missing Pat and the comfort she had brought me. I hoped it was not the last time I would ever see her.

I steered Lumen onward, past the village, and we began our journey once more. I'd checked the compass in the privacy of Pat's home before setting out, the desire needle pointed firmly north, indicating that what I desired most - the weapon to destroy the Shadow Warden - lay in that direction.

Lumen seemed eager to get away from the village, especially as it was so close to the forest where those blood-hungry hounds lurked. I couldn't begin to imagine what it must be like, living so close to it - the constant fear. Pat had told me last night that people never left the village alone, only in groups of four at the least, and always in protective gear. I think all three of us appreciated the wide, open fields ahead of us - easy to survey our surroundings and spot an attack miles before it could happen. Flat, rolling plains tumbled before us, but ahead I could see the hazy outline of another forest that we would have to enter into soon. I hoped that one contained fewer hounds.

Lumen galloped in short bursts, flying effortlessly across the fields. I reined her in to a walk to let her recover, but it was only minutes before she broke into a sprint once more. Sylas and I shared our lunch on Lumen's back, and I leant forward to feed her strips of beef from my sandwich. I was stunned once again when I went to take a drink from the gourd, which had been practically empty yesterday, and found it full to the brim. Self-replenishing, of course. I didn't share my surprise with Sylas this time as he seemed to be unfazed by it all.

Before long, the line of trees forming the forest began to gain clarity as we drew closer. Goosebumps prickled along my back. I wasn't ready to be back in such an enclosed space, with the trees so close again. Not after our harrowing near-death experience with the hounds. But we didn't have a choice. The forest stretched on for miles either side, and it would waste too much time trying to avoid it.

'Let's go through there,' Sylas's voice came from behind me, and I followed the direction of his finger. He was pointing at a path weaving through the forest, flanked by large, mossy rocks on either side that created a narrow trail between them. If Sylas kept an eye behind, and I forward, then nothing could sneak up on us or take us unaware. Even so, as we entered the trail, I slid the dagger from my boot, feeling safer with it clutched in my palm.

The forest was peaceful. Large leaves drifted gently onto the sun-drenched floor. Lumen picked her way gracefully over tree roots clawing their way out of the ground and rocks jutting into the winding path. It was slower than cutting straight through the forest, but I didn't like the idea of being watched from the thick of the ferns again. This felt safer.

That was until we rounded a corner and startled a deer, which leapt into the air and took off at a run. Lumen, who was on edge already, panicked and reared, throwing Sylas and I backwards. I slid off the saddle and tried to roll myself into a ball with my arms over my head as the ground loomed. I hit the floor with such force that the air inside my lungs collapsed. I lay there, winded, trying to gather enough breath back into my body. It took several heart-pounding seconds until I recovered myself.

Lumen thrashed her head wildly before she eventually calmed herself down. She approached me solemnly and nuzzled at my ear as an apology.

'It's okay, I'm all good, girl.'

'Are you hurt?' Sylas said, getting to his feet and examining me with his eyes. He held out a hand and I took it, groaning at the dull ache in my ankle.

'Yeah, I'm good, just hit my ankle at a weird angle but I'll live. You good?'

'I'm fine. Bloody horse,' Sylas said, the grumpy demeanour he had been slowly shedding clouding over him once again.

'It's not her fault,' I retorted, jumping to her rescue. I gave Lumen a tender pat to reassure her. 'She's jumpy from almost being eaten alive yesterday. In fact, we all would have been eaten alive if she hadn't saved us. So reel in the attitude. Let's go.'

I tenderly mounted Lumen again. 'Ah, the pack, I almost forgot. It rolled off my back when I fell. Could you grab it - it's just there, wedged under the rock. See?'

Sylas grabbed the pack, and the moment he pulled the strap, his face contorted with pain before quickly returning to a blank expression. It was only then that I noticed he held his wrist at an odd angle.

'You *are* hurt,' I said accusingly. He tucked the wrist behind his back and handed me the pack with the other.

'No, as I said, I'm fine. Nothing a man like me can't handle,' he said, putting a hand on Lumen's saddle in preparation to mount. He winced ever so slightly.

I put a hand to his chest, pushing him back down. 'No, you're not. Let me see.' I held out a hand expectantly.

'Aurora -'

'Let me see. *Now*,' I said impatiently. He rolled his eyes but gently placed his wrist in my hand. It felt hot to the touch, and I could already see it was starting to swell. I prodded it slightly and Sylas bit his lip.

'It's sprained,' I sighed. Great, just what we needed. 'Why didn't you tuck and roll like me?'

Sylas pulled his hand back, cradling his wrist defensively. 'So sorry, I was too busy falling to my death to think, *oh yeah, I should tuck and roll like good old Aurora*,' he tutted. 'Anyway, there's nothing to be done, so let's just get on with it.'

He managed to mount Lumen with a hiss of pain, quickly stifled by a cough. But he was wrong - there *was* something we could do about it. As part of my assassin training, we'd been taught how to heal ourselves if injured in a fight, even without medical supplies, using only nature's bare materials. I waited until we exited the narrow passageway and the forest opened up before us, then slid off the saddle to examine the ground.

'Did you bang your head earlier or something?' Sylas asked.

'No, why?' I said, without lifting my eyes from the ground.

'Well, it's just that you got off the horse to stare at the ground for no reason.' Sylas's voice dripped with sarcasm.

I didn't bother replying as I spotted what I was looking for - two sturdy sticks, both roughly equal in length. Sylas had dismounted Lumen now to come over and watch me. I took the strip of material from my pocket that Sylas had given me yesterday to clean the hound's blood with.

'Hold out your wrist,' I instructed. His eyebrows furrowed at the request, but he did so, I took his wrist gently and placed the two sticks either side, bounding the material around them to hold it in place. It must have hurt, even though I was being careful, but he just watched me as I worked. Once I was done, I looked up, my eyes clashing with his brown-green ones. He dropped his gaze quickly to his wrist, turning it this way and that to examine my work.

'It holds your wrist in place,' I explained. 'So you can't move it too much from now. Try to only use your other hand. The swelling will go in a few days if you are careful with it.'

He nodded obediently. 'Thank you.'

'No problem. Right, let's have a little break then. Lumen's thirsty. Do you want some water, girl?' I said, diving into the pack. I cursed. The gourd water bottle was smashed into pieces. I guessed it had shattered from the fall earlier.

I dumped out the broken pieces on the floor. I knew that I could fashion another water bottle later if I found the right materials, but once again it meant more of our precious time being spent on trivial matters, rather than moving along.

'Let's just rest for the moment, we can worry about finding water later,' Sylas said. He dropped to his knees, then rolled onto his back, resting on the moss-carpeted floor with his good hand behind his head and the sprained one resting on his stomach, gazing up at the canopy above. I took a deep breath. He was right – let's deal with one issue at a time. I hauled myself up onto a fallen tree nearby.

I took in the forest, the dappled sunlight streaming through the leaves of the twisted, moss-covered oaks, the green leaves that shivered in unison with the soft blow of the wind. I wished my parents could see this. Most people in Nexonia would never get to see this natural kind of beauty in their lifetime, our land was so crammed and populated that everywhere you looked was building and cobblestone. Of course there were trees, but few and far between.

'Penny for your thoughts?' Sylas's voice broke my wandering mind. He was tossing a coin in his hand.

'I was just thinking about your lack of survival skills. It's truly shocking.'

Sylas cocked his head to one side, studying me. 'Come on, tell me. We are stuck with each other for a month so might as well get to know one another a bit.'

'I was… well, I was thinking about my parents. How I think they would like this view,' I admitted. My cheeks felt hot. Before I knew it, the penny came flying at me. I caught it just before it smacked me in the face and tutted at Sylas, who let out a low, rumbling laugh. 'Your turn,' I said. The smile faltered and he turned his eyes to the sky.

'I guess I am excited to not have to watch my back constantly when this mission is over.'

Right. He was looking forward to the mission being over. I don't know why the words stung me a little, but they did. But then I suppose I was feeling the same way, the sooner I could get back to my family, the better.

Sylas seemed to read my face. 'What are they like? Your parents?'

I struggled to find words that could capture the love I felt for them. 'Honestly, they mean everything to me. My Pa - he's the best I could ever ask for. When I was young, I always felt different from other girls. I loved fighting, climbing, I was always coming home with banged up knees from getting into some kind of trouble. Boys get praised for that, for being tough, for becoming "men". But as a girl, I was just met with tuts and shaking heads. Except from my Pa. He was never ashamed of me. In fact, he's the one who pushed me to serve the Queen, to join the assassin team and put my unique skills to use to protect Nexonia.

'And my Ma...' Just thinking of her made me smile. 'She's an angel. She was always the one cleaning up my cuts and bruises when I came home crying, giving me kisses on the nose. There've been days when the weight of what I do, the killing, the choices I've made, feels like too much to bear. And somehow, she always knows. She'll come over and wrap me in a hug and remind me I'm not a bad person. That I'm protecting our land. That I'm keeping it safe from civil war.'

I stopped talking then, because the notion of not being able to save them made my heart throb. My jaw ached as I held in tears. I would not let myself be vulnerable in front of a boy ever again. I learned my lesson the last time. I decided that my hair had become very interesting and studied it.

Sylas didn't attempt to comfort me, perhaps sensing this would embarrass me even more, but he said, 'They will live. We will get the Divinal Stone.'

I tossed my plait aside. 'What about you? What are your parents like?'

Sylas sucked his teeth. For a moment he was silent, and I wondered if he would answer at all.

'My father died when I was very young. I don't remember him so I'm not that sad about it, I know that sounds harsh but it's the truth. My mother… she's as good as dead to me. I used to look up to her. Admire her. Wanted to be as headstrong and fierce as she was. But it turns out she's not someone I would ever look up to anymore. So… yeah.'

He nodded his head awkwardly. I didn't know what to say, so without thinking, I launched the penny back at him. He clocked it flying at his face too late to catch it and just about jerked his head out the way.

'What was that for?' He stared open mouthed. I couldn't help but snort at the expression on his face.

'We both shared our thoughts, so you deserve the penny back.'

He rolled his beautiful eyes but smiled softly, tucking the penny back into his cloak. We sat in silence for another beat, soaking in the personal words we had shared with one another. I felt lucky to have a family I would do anything for; to fight for, to die for. I couldn't imagine not having that familial support, people who were in your corner no matter the circumstances. When I had my heart broken, my parents had been there for me, picking up the pieces and slotting them back together.

Which is exactly why I had to save them.

Chapter Nine

The ground staggered upwards in a steep incline. We could have avoided the hill, but Sylas and I had agreed it would be beneficial to see the land from above and assess the clearest route to take for our journey. We had dismounted Lumen to take the weight off her back, and we were all puffing and panting by the time we finally reached the top. But the view was worth it.

The sky was dusted with shades of pink and grey, like a piece of art. Ahead, the sprawling landscape was interrupted by a vast, glittering lake, its waters channelled from the sea, carving out a huge chunk of the land. I pulled out the Desire Compass; the desire needle had pointed the same direction all day - strongly north. I couldn't help but notice my heart sink a little as I swept in the expanse of land before us. I couldn't see any sign of a church or, for that matter, any building at all. It looks like we would be sleeping under the stars once again tonight.

'Come on,' Sylas said, nudging me to mount Lumen. He probably read the worry on my face. I returned my face to neutral and climbed into the saddle, Sylas hopped up after, being careful not to put any strain on his left wrist as he did so.

A few hours later, when night had descended, I could see the lake's vast body ahead. The moon peered down from above, its pale face mirrored on the dark surface of the water. Sylas prised the reins from my hands and began to steer Lumen towards the lake.

'What are you doing?' I said, trying to take the reins back.

'We need some water, Lumen's parched. I'm parched.'

'No Sylas, we can't, the woman at the village that I stayed with warned me that we needed to stay clear of bodies of water. *Particularly* large ones,' I snapped, adrenaline starting to pump through my body.

'Aurora, you saw the landscape at the top of the hill. There was no other water source for miles other than this lake. If we don't take full advantage of it now, then we could be in serious trouble.'

'No. I'm not risking it!'

'*You* don't have to. Listen, you can stand well back from the lake whilst Lumen and I have a quick drink, then we can leave straight away. And when you go light-headed and delirious from dehydration later on, then too bad.' He added a playful smile to the last line, softening the jab.

I chewed my lip. Unfortunately, he was right again. Lumen did need a drink; she hadn't had a drop all day and it wasn't fair to her. If we continued without stopping off at the lake, I wasn't sure how much longer we would have to travel until we next came across water. It could be several days - at which point we would all be dead.

Even so, it didn't stop the panic constricting my chest as we got nearer the water. I watched from a few meters away as Sylas approached the lake's edge. He scanned the surface, then picked up a rock and threw it into the lake, watching it for signs of huge jaws and tentacles to emerge. The black water rippled, then calmed.

Sylas shrugged at me before kneeling at the edge, cupping his hands to scoop up water. He brought it down over his neck, scrubbing at the dirt and sweat of the day. I drew my eyes away from him as he doused it over his head, shaking his sodden curls from his eyes. Lumen joined him warily and was soon gulping in the fresh water too. She drank long and deep, Veil knows she deserved it. Sylas saw me watching and smacked his lips.

'Ah, so refreshing,' he teased, a sly grin spreading across his face. 'I was parched but now I feel *great*.'

I heaved a sigh before dropping the pack to the ground, fingers still curled around my dagger as I cautiously approached the water's edge. Sylas stepped back, gesturing to the lake to indicate it was all mine. I knelt down, dipping one finger into the water tentatively. I waited. Nothing happened. I cupped my hands then, greedily spooning the fresh water down my throat. Only now did I realise just how parched I was. I'd never appreciated water more. I dangled over the water's edge, tempted to dunk my head in so I could wash my hair too. That's when a webbed hand shot up from the depths and seized my plait.

I screamed and tried to draw back from the edge, but it was pulling me closer with an iron grip. Thinking fast, I used my dagger to slice my plait, letting the webbed hand come away with a huge chunk of my beautiful hair. I began to scramble back from the edge, my legs kicking me away as I scooted on my bum, but the hand reached right out and gripped my ankle.

It was so *strong*; it clamped down on my ankle and began to drag me closer to the water.

'Aurora!' Sylas yelled, running toward me. I looked back, but just as I stretched out a hand to him, the hand on my ankle yanked me into the icy water. The last thing I saw was Sylas's face, bone-white, as he grasped at the air where I had been moments ago.

I plunged into the water, bubbles bursting from my lips as I shrieked. My hands clawed at the water, but it was useless. I kicked and thrashed, but whatever had me wouldn't let go. I tried to look, to see what was dragging me down, but all I saw was darkness - the abyss pulling me under. The surface of the lake exploded above me as Sylas jumped in, attempting to dive after me. His hand stretched out toward me. But it was too late. I was already becoming part of the darkness of the murky depths.

Even if that thing let go of me now, I was too far under to swim to the surface. Blackness gnawed at the edge of my consciousness, my lungs burned for air, and the world slipped away.

Chapter Ten

The water was inside my lungs. I lurched upwards and retched, water dribbling down my chin. I went to bring a hand up to wipe my mouth, but they wouldn't move. They were restrained.

'Aurora - your alive! Thank the Veil. Oh, thank the Veil!' Sylas's voice bellowed from opposite me, echoing around the dull walls. I managed to lift my head from where I sat slumped against a wall. Sylas was shackled around the ankles and his arms were pinned above his head. Despite this, the look on his face was utter relief.

'Where are we?' I felt groggy, disorientated. Like I'd just woken up from a horrid dream. I dragged my eyes across the room, it was bare, with stony walls and no windows. The only light in the place seeped in from under the barred doors, but other than that, we were in darkness. The glitter of hope in Sylas's eyes extinguished and he shook his head, the curls flopping over his eyes.

'I am so sorry, Aurora. I will get us out of here, I *promise*. I'll talk to them-'

'Talk to who?' I said sharply. Nothing made sense. I had drowned, hadn't I? I had lost consciousness and drowned? Sylas opened his mouth but was interrupted as the door rattled open.

With a shriek, I scrambled back as far as I could from the creature that had just entered. It was unlike anything I had ever seen - a confusing mix of woman and fish. Its pale green skin shimmered iridescently in the dim light, golden fins traced down its bald head and behind its pointed ears. The upper half of the creature resembled a woman, gold armour encased her chest, her skirt was woven from seaweed, and swayed as though still underwater - beneath it were scaled legs that ended in webbed feet. My eyes darted to the webbed hands, just like the ones that had dragged me under and taken me... here. Wherever *here* was.

She locked those wide, icy blue eyes onto me, unblinking and cold.

'Come. It's time to get you ready. Follow me.' Her voice was smooth, almost hypnotic, like a dream teetering on the edge of a nightmare. With a casual wave of her hand, the chains binding my wrists clattered to the ground. But I didn't move.

'Get ready for what?'

Sylas was shaking his head at me. *Don't question them, just go.*

'You're our guests of honour,' the creature said simply. 'Now, come, there isn't much time.'

And she turned to leave down a corridor. I just stared after her.

'Go,' Sylas urged. 'I promised I would get you out of here, but I think we need to go along with whatever they are doing for now - be their guests of honour or whatever. It gives us time to think of a plan.'

I turned my frosty gaze to him. My hands shook, not with cold but with anger. Rising to my feet, I snatched my dagger that had been cast aside and shoved it into my boot. As I walked past Sylas, I stopped at the door to hiss, 'I told you not to go near the water. I *told* you. And you didn't listen.'

The usual boyish charm that danced in his eyes was gone as he muttered, 'I know, Aurora. I am so sorry-'

'Save it,' I cut in, turning on my heel to follow the creature. Her form retreated down the dimly lit hallway, disappearing around a corner. I hurried to catch up, and as I rounded the bend, I found myself in a whole other world.

I was in a corridor made entirely of glass, offering a clear view of the underwater kingdom beyond. In the distance, a towering palace with pearly white pillars, balconies, and domes was illuminated by the moonlight filtering through the murky waters. Around it swayed dark strands of kelp, within which shadowy creatures darted in and out, too far away to make out clearly. The water pressed against the glass walls, creating a low, constant hum that thrummed in my ears. I couldn't decide if I was more mesmerised or terrified.

Probably the latter.

But how in the Veil were we ever going to escape this place? This was their territory. They were adapted to it - fins, webbed feet, the ability to breathe underwater. Sylas and I didn't stand a chance against them. My stomach churned as I continued to follow the creature to the corridor's end.

She tugged on a pearl-inlaid door handle, which opened up into a large room. The back wall was nothing but a vast pane of glass, offering another view of the watery depths, while the other walls gleamed in pearly white. A circular window in the ceiling allowed the chalky moonlight to cast pale patterns across the floor. Aside from a vanity, chair, and full-length mirror, the room was entirely bare. My sodden boots squelched with each step, the only sound in the silent space.

'Take a seat. I will send someone to tend to you in just a moment,' was all the creature said before leaving me.

But as soon as she was gone, I rushed to the door. I waited a beat, pressing my ear against it until her footsteps faded away down the corridor. Now was the time to try and find a way out of here.

I tugged on the handle - it didn't move an inch. Panic rose in my chest. I slammed a palm against it. It was stead-fast. Shit. She must have locked it with whatever powers she possessed. I cursed fiercely under my breath. I rushed over to the wall made entirely of glass instead, pressing a hand against it, feeling the solid form beneath my fingers. The glass itself looked very thick. I pounded a fist against it. Nothing.

I brought down my fist again, even harder, frustration swelling in my stomach. Why hadn't Sylas listened to me? I brought my fist down upon the glass again. Now we were stuck here, in this place, way out of our depth. Literally. Both fists hammered on the glass now, the window taking the full brunt of the anger that was uncoiling inside me like a snake. Why did everyone I trusted other than my parents let me down? I was smashing my fists in rapid succession now, knowing the glass wouldn't break, but I was just so angry I didn't care. The sides of my hands were throbbing, but I didn't care, didn't care, didn't care.

'Would you like to take a seat so we can get started?' a voice called from across the room. I whirled around to see two more of those sea creatures waiting patiently as I raged against the window. Instead of the gold armour the first creature had worn, they wore blue, floaty dresses with puffed sleeves. The ends of the dresses trailed in ragged strips, reminding me of the tentacles of giant squid monsters I had read about in books. These females were not warriors then, like the first one I had met. Perhaps I could fight them? I might stand a chance if they had no combat training.

But what was the use? Even if I defeated them and escaped the room, I would still be trapped in the endless prison of glass corridors. I felt the anger in my body drain away, and I slouched onto the chair for them. Too tired to be wary. They got to work immediately.

I tried to hide my cringe at the webbed hands that worked on me. They began by brushing a powder - created from crushed pearls - over my face, which in turn gave it a healthy shimmer, as though I hadn't been living in the woods and sleeping in trees for days. Next they lined my eyes with sea ink, creating a smoky and seductive look.

They took some scissors and evened out the hair that I had hacked short earlier. Rather than falling to the middle of my back, it now swayed around my shoulders. I reached a hand and touched it tenderly, not used to how light it felt. One of the creatures batted my hand away impatiently and began to comb it through, which took some time, seeing as it had become matted and clumped in the plait I had kept it in from the start of the journey. They scooped it into a bun, leaving out soft tendrils that curled around my face. Mother-of-pearl shell earrings dangled at my neck, perfectly matched by a necklace that accentuated my collarbones.

The creatures turned their backs on me as I was instructed to strip to my underwear, replace my clothes with a dress, and swap my boots for the pale green, flat-toed shoes they had provided. While their backs were turned, I took the opportunity to slip the dagger from my boot and tuck it into my dress, between my breasts. The cold metal bit into my skin, yet its presence was familiar, comforting. Once they had finished, I was finally permitted to look in the mirror. I had to clamp my jaw shut to keep it from hanging. Delicate strands of dark green kelp hugged my body, accentuating my curves before billowing out and sweeping the floor. Woven within were bioluminescent strands that glowed blue, silver, and green, casting a soft light through the depths of the dress.

I couldn't believe how... beautiful I looked. But as I stared at my reflection, my mind shot back to a painful memory I'd buried deep within - a memory I always fought so hard not to remember. The only other time I'd ever allowed myself to dress up like this.

It had been for him... Cain.

I had met Cain when I was fifteen, before I started my assassin training. He sat a couple of rows ahead of me in school - dark skin, closely cropped hair, black almond-shaped eyes, and a cheeky smile that tugged at the corner of his mouth. I still remember the first time he glanced back, and our eyes met. A strange, twisting pit of nerves formed in my stomach - something I'd never felt before.

Sure, I'd had little crushes before, but they were always one-sided. I was too rough around the edges, too eager to fight, climb, and do all the things that weren't considered 'proper' for girls in Nexonia. So when Cain showed an interest in me, I was desperate to impress him.

When the summer fair came around, I decided it was my chance. I stuffed myself into a flouncy dress, wrestled with my fiery hair to make it presentable, and tried to look... softer. More delicate. I wanted to be what he wanted.

But on my way to the fair, I saw him in an alley with another girl. She was everything I wasn't - delicate, graceful, effortlessly *feminine*. It came so naturally to her. And there he was, my Cain, with his arms around her, pressing his lips to hers.

And I swear by the Veil, in that moment my fifteen-year-old world shattered. It was like watching my heart break into tiny, irreparable pieces. I stood there, frozen, cheeks burning in my stupid dress.

After that, something inside me hardened. I know it sounds dramatic, but I swore I'd never let anyone have that kind of power over me again. I'd *never* force myself to become someone I wasn't just to win someone's affection.

From that day on, everything I did was either for myself or my family. I wasn't the type to fall in love or dream of having children of my own - and that was fine. I never wanted that life. It was freeing for me, to never care about how I looked. I knew the potential was there, hidden beneath my tough exterior and baggy clothes, but I didn't need it. I hadn't even thought about it... until now.

Behind me the two creatures nodded to one another approvingly, then left without a word. As soon as the door closed, my sense of awe at my transformation thawed and I was back into survival mode. Why were they dressing me up; what were Sylas and I guests of honour for? I was left asking myself these questions until the door opened again. I was so on edge that I jumped. The creature who had led me from the prison appeared, but her golden armour had been replaced, as she was now in a long sapphire dress, carefully embroidered with golden thread that resembled waves.

She beckoned me to follow her through another round of glassy corridors until we eventually reached a set of massive iron doors. The muffled sound of noise and chaos seeped from behind them, and the moment she pushed them open, it hit me.

The room was enormous. Two long tables stretched from one end to the other, lined with hundreds of those sea creatures, all dressed in various hues of green and blue. Their chatter filled the space with a constant murmur, like the ebb and flow of gentle ripples. The walls were mostly arched windows which boasted the view of the underwater kingdom's grounds. Everything was magnificent, but it was the ceiling that stole my breath away. Strands of kelp and seaweed draped down from above, woven with the same bioluminescent threads as my dress, casting an ethereal blue light across the room.

At the far end of the hall, seated on a throne made of shimmering pearl, sat who could only be deduced as the King of this palace.

As I was led down the centre isle towards the King, I felt icy eyes collecting on me. Their guest of honour. I spotted Sylas at the other end of one of the long tables, an empty seat beside him for me. Our eyes locked, and his widened as he took me in, his mouth slightly ajar. I held that gaze, the confidence of knowing my beauty. But my own stare was only hard and cold in return.

It wasn't until I was right before him that he seemed to break from his trance, shaking his head quickly. I couldn't help but notice how devastatingly handsome he looked. His usually untidy hair had been styled into neat curls for once, and like the other males in the room, he wore a thin white shirt that clung to his form, showing off the intricate gold paint swirling across his chest. He wore dark green trousers that fit perfectly, paired with polished black shoes adorned with a shell buckle.

'Take a seat. The feast will begin shortly,' the creature said, gesturing to the seat beside Sylas, and I obeyed. Before either of us had a chance to exchange a word, the King clapped his hands and servants came pouring from the side doors, laying the tables with dish after dish. Soon the table was heaving with grilled fish, seasoned with underwater herbs, platters upon platters of oysters and muscles, crab, lobster, algae-based soups, coral-crusted cakes, caviar, a variety of fruits that I had never heard of that had been harvested underwater. Goblets were topped up with a swirling acid-green liquid, which I didn't touch.

The servants offered us plate after plate, and I shook or nodded my head according to what looked vaguely similar to our normal human food. Their servings were huge, and my plate soon towered in front of me precariously. Everyone was tucking in, so I took my fork and reluctantly speared some fish. I nibbled on a piece as I observed the dining room, trying to mark all the exits, but soon the plate consumed my attention. The food was so warm, so *fresh*. Each bite was an explosion of herbs and flavours in my mouth, and I couldn't get enough. I reached for the goblet to inspect the drink inside and Sylas flinched.

'What happened to your hand?' he said, his eyebrows furrowed deeply. I turned my hand to see, violent purple bruises blossomed along the side. Sylas's knuckles were white around his fork. 'Did they do that to you?'

'No,' I said quietly, my voice deadly. '*I* did that. When I was trying to escape by breaking the glass.'

Sylas's face turned dark. 'I am so sorry, Aurora. I promised I would get-'

'Yeah, you already said that.' My insides cringed at the look of pure sorrow on his face. I carried on with my meal, ignoring him as he fidgeted beside me, clearly guilty at the situation he had got us into. There was no escaping this place. We were outnumbered by the hundred, the glass was much too thick to crack, not to mention there were many eyes on us. The guests of honour.

I couldn't finish my meal and had to turn down dessert. I was starting to feel sick with dread. Something bad was going to happen, I could feel it grinding at my bones. Sylas and I sat there amongst the roar of chatter, breathing hard. I wanted to get out of here. Now. I hadn't noticed my knee trembling until Sylas placed a gentle hand on it to steady it.

'Don't,' I said, moving my leg.

I started as the King rose from the throne and cleared his throat, the room fell silent at once, the last noise echoing into stillness.

'Good evening all my fellow Nautlian's. It is so lovely to be gathered here today once again, and I hope you all thoroughly enjoyed the feast. Now we move onto the long-awaited part of our night - the entertainment! Our lovely guests of honour here,' the King swept a hand towards us and all eyes swivelled our way, 'will be taking part in tonight's entertainment, so I do hope you enjoy. Without further ado, I ask that you all make your way to the entertainment room and we shall get started!'

Entertainment. The word rattled around in my skull. We were their entertainment.

Chairs scraped against the marble floors as the Nautlian's rose and headed back through the main doors to the entertainment room - wherever that was.

The sea creature - Nautlian - in the sapphire dress strolled over.

'I suggest you drink up. It's an insult to leave your goblet empty here,' she said, her eyes boring into us. I hesitated and she twirled the spear she now held in her hands menacingly. A threat. Sylas and I drank up reluctantly. It was a salty, gritty mixture, much like licking the bottom of the sea. I barely managed to take it all in before a wave of nausea rolled through me, and I placed a hand on my stomach, feeling as though I might wretch it all back up.

But I didn't have time to dwell on the horrific taste, because the Nautlian was now ushering me to follow her. We did so, but she turned and held out a hand to stop Sylas.

'Not you, only the girl. Another Nautlian will come for you,' she said to Sylas. She gestured toward a doorway, and as I walked toward it, she followed closely behind me. Just before I stepped through, I glanced over the Nautlian's shoulder to see Sylas standing there, panic etched across his face. Why weren't we following the other Nautlian's to the entertainment room? Had they changed their minds?

I entered into a small room, the thick walls creating a muffled silence that enveloped me. The Nautlian propped her spear to the wall and extracted a small knife from the pocket of her dress. My blood began pumping in my ears, I raised my fists, ready to fight. Ready to fight until my last dying breath. But she rolled her eyes.

'Stop bouncing on your feet. I'm not trying to kill you, if I wanted to do that, I would have used my spear.'

I slowly dropped my fists. Without a word, she grasped the hem of my dress and sliced through the kelp, shortening it so that it no longer trailed behind me but stopped half-way up my thigh.

'What are you doing?' I said, stepping away.

'The King said we at least need to give you a chance to fight for a while, otherwise it will be boring. You can't hope to survive for even a moment in a dress that long, and you will need to be able to move your legs to swim. We need to give the Elite Nautlian's something to watch.'

The King was making sure I was able to move easier - to *fight* something? He didn't want the fight to end too quickly. No, he wanted some kind of a show. I never liked showing fear, but right now, I couldn't stop my body from shaking.

'Why are you doing this? Why can't you just let us go?' I sniped. The Nautlian seemed unbothered, and her shoulders rose.

'It's out of principle. The people who drink from our waters must pay the price. And you are unlucky enough to have drunk from our lake on our entertainment night, when the Elite Nautlian's come together to be amused for the evening. The King likes to keep them happy, and you were the perfect opportunity for that. We haven't had anyone foolish enough to drink from our waters in years.'

'We didn't know, honestly. There was no disrespect intended.' I hated how pleading my voice sounded, so I quickly hardened it. 'Let us go.'

The Nautlian smiled at my demand. 'You've got some nerve; I'll give you that. But it's too late. It's showtime.' She moved past me and opened a second door, guiding me through with a firm, webbed hand on my back.

The minute I stepped out the room, the crowd's cheers erupted from below.

I was in the entertainment room.

Chapter Eleven

I found myself on a raised platform, looking down at a cheering crowd of Nautlian's. In the centre of the room was a large glass tank, with a plank extending from my platform toward its middle. On the opposite side of the room, an identical plank stretched toward the tank's centre. The two planks almost met, but a gap remained between them, dropping directly into the tank below.

The tank itself was filled to the brim with grimy water, so thick you could only just about make out the dark rocks and seaweed within. The Nautlian pushed me forward firmly. They wanted me to walk the plank and jump into that tank.

No.

No, no, no.

I stopped moving my feet, grasping at the low railing either side of the plank. The forceful hand on my back became a sharp spear point. She jabbed it into my back, making me leap forward. I nearly lost my balance right there, which would have sent me plummeting several hundred feet into the hungry crowd of Nautlian's below. It would serve them right, to have my blood and guts caked all over them. I looked back to see the Nautlian edging nearer, bracing the spear.

'Move, girl,' she hissed at me.

What was I going to do? I took tiny steps forward, trying my best to prolong the little time I had left until I reached the end. Movement in front of me had me whipping my head up. Sylas was being prodded along the other plank, we were both sidling closer and closer to the edge. Into the tank.

My mind was whirring. I could stop moving. Let them slowly impale me to death right here. It would be better than dealing with whatever lurked in that tank, surely? Better than being the Nautlian's gruelling entertainment for tonight?

But something within me wouldn't let that happen. Even if death was certain in the tank, it gave me more time - even if it was only a few minutes longer - to try and think of a plan as I edged closer to the end.

There was nowhere else to go. I couldn't go back. I couldn't jump from the sides. Only forward.

And then down.

Into the water.

My toe kissed the edge of the plank.

There was a roaring in my ears, not from the chanting crowd, but the anger and pain welling up inside. Those emotions I was all too familiar with. The air crackled with excitement down below. They were ready for a show.

My eyes searched the crowd, and I located the King seated comfortably at the head of the tank, watching his Nautlian's with a smile on his face. He wanted them to be entertained. With blood. Gore. Pain.

There was another sharp jab to my back. This time it penetrated my skin and I felt thick, hot liquid trickle down my spine. Sylas had also reached the end of his plank, and I looked up at him, knowing my eyes were filled with fear. I didn't care anymore. What was the use of the tough exterior I always wore now? Between us was nothing but murky water and whatever skulked in that tank.

'You have twenty minutes until the potion wears off, and your breathing returns to normal,' the Nautlian hissed behind me. I opened my mouth to ask what she meant, but then it hit me. The *drink* - the one she had forced us to down. The memory of that salty mixture made my whole body shudder. They must have laced it with a potion to allow us to breathe underwater, just long enough to make the fight more entertaining. She hissed again, 'Now jump.'

My breath was shallow in my chest. The dark water below waited, and within something awful lurked. The Nautlian's were eager to watch it torment us, tear us apart, kill us.

'On three?'

I tore my eyes away from the death lurking beneath to meet Sylas's gaze.

'We can't, Sylas. The minute we jump in we're dead,' I panted. I was going to be sick. Sylas reached out across the gap between us and took my hand. He gripped it tightly as he leaned in close.

'This is not the end, Aurora. I won't let it be.'

My breath shuddered in my chest.

'Ready?' Sylas asked, giving my hand a squeeze. I was never going to be ready, but I nodded. I stole one last glance at the King, and if looks could kill, his heart would have ceased its beating right then. 'Three...two...*one*.'

At that, we both jumped. Air whistled in my ears, mingling with the crowd's erupting screams, but all that noise died the instant we hit the water. Sylas kept a firm hold on my hand as we plunged into the murky depths, the icy water leaching into my veins. My body felt foreign with the potion in my system, every nerve tingled.

Without thinking, I opened my mouth, accidentally swallowing a mouthful of the foul water. Panic filled my body as I began to choke underwater, grasping at my neck, but Sylas's grip tightened on my hand. Grounding me. Reminding me we can breathe. I forced my heart to slow and took a breath - a real breath. It was the strangest sensation when the water didn't rush into my nose. I could breathe it in, just like oxygen.

But we only had twenty minutes. Twenty minutes... to fight what?

I scanned the gloomy depths. The water was a greenish murk, so thick we couldn't see more than fifty meters ahead. We both trod water, trying to gather our bearings. Below were rocks, caves, narrow crevices, and thick swaying seaweed. Sylas tugged my arm, pointing to a small cave in the side of a rock formation, just big enough for both of us to squeeze into. A good place to hide whilst we figured out some kind of a plan. We kicked our way toward it as fast as we could.

From one side of the tank, I could see the faces of the Elite Nautlian's

78

pressed against the glass, all jostling one another out the way for the best view. I felt pathetic, powerless. They were watching us like we were mice stuck in a cage with a lion.

Once we reached the cave, Sylas stuck his head in, checking every corner to see if it was safe to enter. He nodded and I squeezed through the thin entrance, tucking myself into the far corner so Sylas could follow. I wondered if we stayed here long enough that the creature in the tank with us - wherever it was - might get impatient and just leave us alone. Unlikely. It would probably wait until we ran out of air, then come straight for us the instant we emerged for the surface.

It was as Sylas began to squeeze himself into the cave beside me that I saw it.

Emerging from the darkness, something massive came hurtling toward him with terrifying speed - a single bulbous, milky eye loomed, pale and gleaming. Then I saw the mouth: gaping, a cavernous tunnel lined with bone and cartilage, stuffed with hundreds of teeth like razors. A giant slaughterfish. Its body must have been at least three times the length of my own.

I screamed, useless bubbles streaming from my mouth. Sylas turned to look, but I knew that wouldn't give him enough time to react, so with both hands I grabbed Sylas's shoulders and dragged him into the safety of the cave. His body had only just fit through the jutting rocks when the slaughterfish's jaws snapped at the narrow entrance. It was just inches from tearing us apart, only held back by the thin slice of rock. I could see right into the back of its mouth, a never-ending pit of darkness and death beyond those teeth. Its white eye lingered on us, watching intently before it swerved away and retreated into the darkness. Waiting for us to make our next move.

I was paralysed, staring into the spot where it had disappeared. My heart pounded furiously against my chest. We had to fight *that*? I pressed myself further back into the crevice of the cave, and my movement stirred something beneath me. Something white scuttled along the floor. I glanced down.

Bones.

The remains of the other "guests of honour" who had chosen drowning to be more favourable than being devoured by the slaughterfish. Sylas's face was as pale as those remains as I looked over at him. He'd been seconds away from being swallowed whole. I didn't know what to do. My mind whirred, thoughts crashing and tumbling over one another, but no solution came.

The slaughterfish had every advantage - it was born to be in the water. Aside from the temporary effects of the potion, we had nothing going for us other than our own wit.

I pulled the dagger from my dress. I didn't know exactly what to do with it, but having it in my hand felt better than having nothing. Sylas's eyes fixated on the blade, his expression sharpening as he knelt and began to sift through the bones. His hand wrapped around one, a femur, if I had to guess. He looked up, extending his hand and jerking his head at the dagger. I had no idea what he was up to, but I handed it over, and immediately he began to carve the bone with the blade. I watched as he worked, whittling the edge until it was sharp and pointed - a makeshift spear. One weapon became two. Now, at least, we were both armed.

He straightened up, handing me back the dagger and holding his newly crafted spear before he peeked out of the cave, scanning the surroundings. He mouthed, *Wait*, then made to swim out, but I grabbed his shoulder, shaking my head. *What are you doing?* He mimed a ticking motion, indicating to me that we didn't have much time left. It was true - we had wasted nearly five minutes in this cave already.

He squeezed through the gap and swam out into the depths, bracing the spear as he turned in slow circles, monitoring the darkness that surrounded him. The water was still. I could still see the Nautlian's faces pressed against the glass, their eyes searching for the slaughterfish to take its bait. Sylas turned to me with confusion written across his face, and the moment our eyes connected I saw the slaughterfish slide out from the shadows again. I bellowed out, my shouts swallowed up by the water, but it gave Sylas enough warning to turn and dodge as the slaughterfish's body powered right past him. It circled back around, ready for another attack.

As the creature sped toward him, Sylas braced his spear, ready to stab it, but the slaughterfish swerved past it by mere inches. It started to repeat the same movements, pummelling its tail through the water and heading right at Sylas, up until the last moment when it would swerve.

It was playing with its food.

I knew it could kill us easily - the spear wouldn't even scratch it if it decided to swallow Sylas whole. But this is why the King used it to entertain his Nautlian's; because the slaughterfish promised a slow and teasing death.

It would taunt us until our air ran out, and as soon as we surfaced for more, it would drag us down and devour us whole. I wouldn't - *couldn't* - let that happen. Enough was enough.

Whilst the slaughterfish was distracted torturing Sylas, I slid out of the cave, gliding silently into the cover of the seaweed below. I pushed apart the slimy strands, weaving in and out of various rocks, all the while gazing above to check on Sylas. I positioned myself right below him and waited patiently. I hoped the slaughterfish couldn't hear the pounding beat of my heart through the water. This plan could go very, very wrong. But we had no other plan, it was the best I had.

I watched as the slaughterfish prepared to rally again, launching itself at Sylas, and I pushed off the ground as hard as I could. Just as it glided past, I levelled with it and drove my dagger into its massive orb-like eye, tearing straight through the retina. Instantly, white, viscous fluid clouded the water around us. The creature thrashed violently, its tail pounding and stirring up waves, trailing a gooey white substance as it convulsed in pain.

I swam backward toward Sylas as the slaughterfish struggled, and he clutched my arm as that thing started to swim again. But this time, it was different. Its movements were jerky, disorientated. We froze as it swam straight at us, yet it veered off at the last moment, smashing into the side of the glass tank which made the whole thing shudder. Veil above.

I had blinded it.

Up close, the sight was gruesome - the white fluid was slowly turning red and clotted, with strands of shredded tissue hanging where its eye had been. I couldn't help myself; I retched.

The noise caused the slaughterfish to stop in its tracks, and it turned toward us. Now that it had no sight, it was relying on its hearing. White and crimson bled into one as it launched its body towards us. It was done playing now.

Sylas and I dodged separate ways, but I was too slow. I felt a pain, so sharp, so refined, pierce my left arm as the slaughterfish's tooth caught my flesh. More bubbles billowed from my mouth as I brought my arm up to see a long gash where it had sliced me. The water around me turned crimson. Shit.

I needed to concentrate. And I had another idea. There was no way to communicate to Sylas what that idea was, so I could only hope he would observe and understand what I was attempting to achieve.

I swam as fast as I could to the edge of the glass tank. The Nautlian's faces looked eerie as they stared from the other side, their eyes gleaming at the blood streaming from my arm. I reckoned we only had ten precious minutes left of air by now. The slaughterfish had submerged back into the dark depths once again. I needed to draw it out. With the hard metal base of my dagger, I smashed against the glass.

Of course - being far too thick to break from the force of my blows alone - the glass didn't budge. But almost immediately, the slaughterfish was diving towards me, drawn by the vibrations of metal against glass. I kept tapping, guiding it closer to the right spot. Just as it closed in, its enormous mouth gaping, I swerved, mimicking its own tactic. It crashed into the glass, momentarily dazing itself. I floated still and silent beside it as it shook off the impact and turned to swim away again, into the safety of the darkness. I tapped again at the same spot, drawing it back.

The slaughterfish turned violently and plunged again, smashing straight into the glass once more. This time, I heard a splintering noise, and when the slaughterfish swam away, I noticed a tiny crack had formed. The Nautlian's on the other side had the sense to stand back, shocked.

Something registered in Sylas's eyes as they met mine, and he gave me a small nod before swimming a little way beneath me, spear at the ready. On my third tap against the glass, as the slaughterfish barrelled forward, smashing into the glass, Sylas struck upward, driving his bone spear into the monster's stomach. I hadn't realised the slaughterfish could make sound until I was clamping my hands over my ears, desperate to block out the hollow, seething screech it unleashed, vibrating through the water.

When I opened my eyes again, the crack had spread further. My heart pounded faster. This could work. If it kept ramming the glass, with Sylas weakening it from below, the glass might eventually shatter which would send the Nautlian's scattering. Maybe, in the chaos, Sylas and I could escape. I tapped on the glass a fourth time.

But something had changed.

This time, the slaughterfish didn't charge forward - instead it began swimming toward me, *slowly*. Its gaping mouth loomed closer, and its damaged eye, with bloodied tendrils hanging loose, pointed in my direction. It wasn't going to ram the glass anymore; it was hunting us down. And this time I doubt it would play around with us. It was going in for the kill.

Sylas clocked it working its way towards me. He jerked his head slightly, signalling for me to move away slowly, so as not to disturb the water and alert the slaughterfish to my presence. But I ignored him.

And instead swam right towards it.

Straight towards that wide mouth, that pit of darkness. As I got closer, I could see every vertebra in its throat, the endless rows of teeth. I sensed Sylas panicking down below, swimming up to the slaughterfish and stabbing at its tail to distract it, but the monster only ignored him. It could feel my movements, my arm strokes as I glided closer - right into its mouth.

The instant I was inside, its maw tightened around me, those powerful jaws hinging shut. I mustered all the strength I had within me, pouring every emotion I had felt these past few days into my swing as I plunged my dagger upward into the roof of the slaughterfish's mouth, aiming for its brain. I slashed, carving a long, brutal stroke. I tore it apart from the inside, biting back a scream as its teeth became lodged into my arm, tearing my flesh like parchment. And yet I kept going deeper, thrusting up through the roof of the fish's mouth and into its brain. My hand went straight through flesh, into a gooey centre.

A guttural choking sound echoed from deep within that pit of darkness. I had done it. I had reached its brain and I was killing it. The light around me began to fade as the slaughterfish's mouth continued to close around me.

Now that I'd impaled its brain, it could no longer function, no longer stay afloat. It was sinking, and it was taking me with it. I needed to get out. Now.

I pulled my arm back, roaring as the creature's teeth, lodged deep into my flesh, tore free from its gums and embedded themselves into my arm.

I felt a sensation run through my body, the ease of breathing underwater beginning to falter. There was now just a tiny sliver of light coming through the creature's still-parted jaws and I swam toward it as fast as I could, needing to escape before they closed completely. I pushed a hand through, and another hand clasped mine. Sylas pulled me through the fish's jaws right before they snapped shut forever. I realised I'd have to hold my breath from now on; the twenty minutes were up. The potion had fully worn off.

We kicked hard towards the surface, towards the air, the light, the freedom. I dared one last look down and saw the wrecked, milky eye staring sightlessly as it descended into the bottomless depths below.

I broke the surface, and air had never felt so good in my lungs.

Chapter Twelve

I stood in a pool of water and my own blood before the King. I didn't dare look down at the needle-like teeth embedded in my arm. I didn't want to see how many were lodged there, didn't want to risk losing consciousness.

I only stared into his eyes, dark and stormy like thunderous waters. His long, white beard twitched as he surveyed us, trying to figure out how two humans had managed to kill a monster like the slaughterfish.

Sheer determination and anger - that's how we had done it. At least, that's how I did.

Behind us, his precious Nautlian's gathered, whispering among themselves.

'So, you have killed my slaughterfish,' the King's voice rumbled through my chest, silencing the murmur of the crowd. 'That slaughterfish has been our source of entertainment for over one hundred and fifty years. Now I shall have to seek a replacement.'

Sylas's grip tightened on mine. He hadn't let go of my hand since we'd emerged from the tank to face the hundreds of confused faces of the Nautlian's. I swallowed, unsure what to say; it was clear that the King's main concern was keeping his subjects entertained, and we had ruined that.

Sylas cleared his throat. 'Your Majesty, if I may, your Nautlian's deserve more than the slaughterfish,' he said. I nearly lost control of my bladder as the King's lip curled in displeasure. 'Watching the same entertainment for a hundred and fifty years must get tiresome, no? I think it's *good* we killed the monster; we put on one incredible show. And we didn't come away

85

unscathed.' He indicated to my arm, which was thankfully still numb from all the adrenaline pumping through my body. I silently prayed the numbness would last; I wasn't ready to face the pain that was sure to come.

The King's gaze swept over me. I rearranged my expression to look traumatised, letting my lip tremble and my eyes turn hollow.

Sylas continued, 'You wanted a show, and we gave you one. Perhaps it's time to find a new monster for your guests of honour to fight, something fresh and exciting. But we won, fair and square, despite all the odds stacked against us. It's time you let us go, or show yourself as dishonourable before your Nautlian's.'

I sucked in a breath at the tone of the last line. Bold, confident, and unyielding. Sylas didn't break eye contact with the King's steely glare. I half-expected him to waver under the pressure, but he held his ground, his hand warm in mine.

The King finally lifted his head, addressing the room instead. The Nautlian's shuffled closer as their ruler turned his attention toward them. I could feel my heartbeat in my ears as I waited for his response. The King lengthened his back on his throne and rolled his shoulders.

'As you all saw, our guests of honour fought bravely against the slaughterfish tonight. I cannot say I've ever witnessed a victory in this challenge, nor ever thought I'd live long enough to see one. So, I have decided that our guests of honour will be freed, as they fought and won fairly.' Murmurs rippled through the crowd - some hesitant boos but mostly approving titters. There was no denying it. We had won. 'I shall let them go on account of completing the task. We wish them well on their journey and advise them to exercise caution when drinking from lakes where they do not belong in future.'

Nautlian's with goblets clutched in their webbed hands raised them high, echoing, 'Hear, hear!'

Relief nearly buckled my knees. He was letting us go. I could have wept right there, but I didn't. Because unlike what I had thought earlier, I was strong. Not powerless.

The King snapped his fingers, and the Nautlian in the sapphire dress approached, bending as he whispered in her ear. She nodded, then gestured for us to follow. As we passed, the King's expression remained unreadable, but I could have sworn he gave the slightest nod - a reluctant acknowledgment of respect. Respect for the two humans who had defeated his creature, unbeaten for years upon years. I wondered what creature he might choose next for his future guests of honour to fight, and shivered. Not my problem.

The Nautlian led Sylas and I through the glassy corridors until we reached a set of pearly white gates. The metal was shaped in swirling patterns, and beyond that the water of the lake flowed freely. It was as if an invisible barrier stopped the water from crashing down through the hallways. The Nautlian swung the gates open for us.

'The King said you could leave, but he didn't say we would help you get to the surface,' the Nautlian stated plainly. She handed Sylas a bag, in which contained our old clothes and shoes. I stepped right up to the wall of water and tried to peer upwards. Far above, I could just make out the faint glimmer of moonlight through the water. I didn't know if we would make it to the surface without a breathing potion - it would be tight. But staying here forever wasn't an option, so we had to try. When I turned, I found Sylas watching me with concern, his eyes straying to my injured arm.

'Are you ready?' I asked him, hiding my arm behind my back. Bit by bit, the chaos of earlier was wearing away from my body, and I was beginning to feel the sharp sting of the teeth lodged in my arm. But I couldn't focus on that right now. All my attention was on getting out of here.

He nodded, biting his lip, and we both turned to face the barrier, drawing what might be our last breath. I inhaled deeply and dove in. Some kind of vacuum pulled me into the lake, and I used every ounce of momentum to propel myself upward, kicking furiously, pounding the water with my legs. My body screamed in protest from the fighting and pain I'd endured, but I didn't stop. Each kick was agonising, my limbs growing numb, but I kept pushing and pushing, stretching my hands toward the surface, desperate to taste the air again.

My lungs burned. The tops of my fingers glowed silver as they rose into the path of moonlight filtering through the water. I was nearly there, so close to breaking free of the water. Every muscle in my body was tight with tension, I was so ready for something to drag me away from my freedom at the last moment, to drag me from the oxygen my lungs were crying out for.

But then, I burst through the surface - coughing and spluttering and laughing and crying.

I paddled to the lip of the lake, and half draped my body over the edge. I heard a whinny and managed to lift my head to see Lumen cantering towards me. She had waited all this time. She tossed her head, stomping profusely.

'It's okay, girl. We're okay,' I croaked. She carefully pulled at my dress between her teeth to help drag me onto the bank. Sylas was behind me, pushing my legs up, and together they managed to haul my exhausted body to the safety of the bank.

It was only then which I felt the last ember of energy leave my body. The pain in my arm was sharpening now, the throbbing growing worse and worse. I still couldn't bring myself to look, because once I saw the damage, I wasn't sure if I could stop myself from vomiting again. Sylas picked me up gently and hauled me onto Lumen. I drooped over the saddle, and he quickly mounted behind me, roping his arms around my middle to keep me up.

'We just need to find some shelter so we can make a fire and warm up, okay Aurora? Stay with me, alright. Stay with me, please,' Sylas begged. I could tell his words were full of contempt - at himself - for having got us in this situation.

I sagged against him, struggling to keep my eyes open as he shook me gently. Waves of pain seared through me, and my vision darkened as I desperately tried to cling to consciousness. I must have lost the thread at some point, because when I next opened my eyes, I found myself surrounded by trees. I was propped against one, the pack cushioning my head. Sylas was adding the final logs to the roaring fire, his eyes darting to me when he realised I was awake.

He rushed over, crouching beside me.

'I've got our clothes drying by the fire as we speak, so we can get you out of this dress and into your warmer clothes soon. But we need to address your arm first, okay?'

He held my arm so tenderly, examining the damage, his face pale as he took it in. That alone told me how bad the wound was. I had to look.

It was one of the worst mistakes I ever made.

Three huge teeth, the size of my finger, were lodged deep in my arm, and a long gash ran almost from wrist to elbow. Beneath the layers of dried blood, the flesh looked disturbingly white. Around the edges of the wounds, raw, blistered tissue gaped open, swollen and revolting. I turned and vomited beside me. I wasn't even sure how I had enough food left in my stomach to be sick.

'I need to pull these out now,' Sylas said gravely after I had recovered. 'Otherwise, they will get infected.'

I rolled my head against the tree trunk, a sob heaving from my chest. I was just so tired. I didn't want to feel this agony anymore. But what sort of pain would my parents feel if I didn't get these teeth out of my arm - if they got infected and I got too sick to carry on with our mission? Would they suffer worse than this? I gritted my teeth.

'I'll do it,' I said, with little conviction. Sylas bit his lip but didn't say anything. He clearly wasn't keen on me doing it myself but didn't want to argue. I clutched my hand around the first tooth, willing myself to be strong. With a deep breath, I yanked hard.

Hot, burning pain seared my very veins, making my body writhe and contort with pain. Sweat poured down my face and I let a scream rip from my throat. I didn't give a shit if it attracted every creature or beast under the sun to us. I couldn't think beyond anything but the agony I was in. My whole focus was narrowed on that harrowing pain that burrowed into my very soul. I had to keep going.

My hand trembled violently as I took hold of the second tooth. Sylas clutched my free hand.

'Squeeze as hard as you can,' he instructed. His eyes were wide with concern. That grumpy exterior he had worn at the start of this journey was completely gone. Sacrificed for this moment.

I gave a half-hearted nod.

The squelch as the tooth came loose sent a white-hot surge through my arm, like molten lava igniting my veins. More bile rose up in my throat, and I turned to the side, letting it escape. My head swam, my vision darkened. I was completely blinded, though I could still hear Sylas's voice as he called my name. He sounded so *scared*. I was on a tightrope between consciousness.

'I can't see, Sylas. I can't-' I faltered. Blood poured from the wound, and a chilling coldness swept through my whole arm. I was losing too much blood; I could feel it. Sylas took my face in his hands and all I could see in the waves of darkness was his brown-green eyes, just inches from mine. They reminded me of the earth and soil, the leaves and trees, grounding me in that moment. Tears rolled down my cheeks.

'I'm going to do it, Aurora. On the count of three, okay? Stay with me, you got this. Three... two-'

He didn't get to one before he pulled the final tooth out.

'You tricked me,' was all I managed to say before the world went black. Under the blanket of stars, I fell into the bliss of a painless place.

Chapter Thirteen

I peeled my eyes open to see a fiery orange sky. So pretty.

Then I was hit with a wave of agonising pain shooting through the length of my arm, and suddenly all the memories came flooding back. My entire arm was stiff with dried blood. While the pain was still intense, it paled in comparison to the torment of that last tooth being pulled free.

'Good morning,' came a soft voice from above. I peered up to see Sylas's face slide into view. I shot up, much too quickly and stars danced around me. I blinked hard.

'Woah, woah, steady. No fast movements for a while,' Sylas instructed, placing two sturdy hands on either side of my shoulders to anchor me. I waited with my eyes pressed shut for the world to stop spinning until I finally re-opened them - to see Sylas grinning broadly.

'Why, you little *shit*,' I raged suddenly. 'You didn't bloody listen when I told you not to go near that damn lake and then you lied during your countdown, and you yanked the tooth out *before* getting to one,' I shouted in his face. He blinked, and then his lips curled downwards as he battled a smile.

I huffed. 'What's so funny?'

'I'm sorry, I'm not laughing. I am actually so angry with myself for putting you in this position and I will never forgive myself. It's just that, I'm happy to see you are alive enough to be mad at me.'

I frowned and his smile eventually dropped.

'I am really sorry, Aurora. I am such an idiot for not listening to you. And when you were pulling out the teeth from your arm last night, all I could think was... *I* deserved that pain, not you. I would have done anything I could to take it from you.'

I didn't know what to say to this very vulnerable confession. I left the silence hanging between us, my gaze dropping to my lap. I eventually sighed, fixing him with an unimpressed expression.

'You look like you really want to kiss me right now,' Sylas said solemnly, though his eyes glimmered with mischief. I rolled my eyes and unsteadily got to my feet. Glancing down, I noticed he'd made a makeshift bandage from the hem of his shirt, binding it tightly around my arm to stop the bleeding. The fabric crackled with dried blood.

I rubbed my hands roughly over my face. 'We should probably get some distance covered today. Make up for all the times we have been captured or injured. How's your wrist?'

Sylas showed me his wrist, no longer bound in the sticks, and flexed it to show it had healed. He helped me mount Lumen, which took a lot of effort on Sylas's end and swearing on mine. I rummaged in the pack and found the Desire Compass, the desire needle instructed us to head north-west from here.

* * *

Lumen seemed reenergised after a night's rest, and we made great distance that day. We all treated ourselves to share the rest of Pat's food before it spoiled, a morale boost each of us needed as much as the next. My whole focus now was on finding this weapon that we needed to destroy the Shadow Warden.

After everything that had happened the past few days, my whole body was alert, my dagger never leaving my hand. We could not afford to keep getting delayed like this, it could cost us the price of getting the Divinal Stone on time, and getting back for the Night of Two Moons.

* * *

We travelled for six days straight, setting traps to catch our food and roasting it over fires. I'd managed to craft a makeshift water bottle by stripping birch bark and tying it together with the laces from my boots. Of course, this one was not self-replenishing, and I was very wary whenever it came time to refill it. I only ever approached shallow trickles of water and avoided any body of water where I could not see the bottom of the floor. I would not make the same mistake twice. We all slept under the stars and woke early each day to cover more distance.

It was a particularly foggy day when we emerged from the forest into a sprawling marshland. A thick mist veiled the terrain, blurring the horizon and making it impossible to see far, which made me nervous. The desire needle on the compass twitched wildly, beckoning us straight ahead.

Rivers knotted around us, forcing us to constantly navigate the winding meanders of the landscape and often backtrack when our path was blocked by water. I clicked to signal Lumen forward, and we rode cautiously, all aware of the dangers that came with such low visibility. It was deathly silent apart from the soft squelches of Lumen's hooves being sucked by the mud below.

I was ready for anything that might leap out of the fog to attack us.

Sylas breathed in sharply behind me and pointed a finger towards a looming black outline. I strained my eyes to make it out - it was a huge cross.

'I think it's a church,' he whispered. My breathing got faster. The weapon might be here. Queen Velraxis had said it was a priest who had worked alongside Merida to help create the weapon to defeat the shadow creature, so it was certainly logical that it might be here.

As we got closer, it turned out Sylas was right, it was a church, and a large chunk of it had crumbled away, leaving a scatter of rocks for us to pick our way over. It looked as though it had once been a proud, beautiful building, with stained glass windows that gleamed faintly in the faltering sunlight. But now, the tall stone walls were gradually succumbing to nature's embrace, ivy clinging to the moss-covered exterior. I glanced down at the compass again. It was pointing directly at the church.

We reached the wide wooden doors and dismounted. I pressed my ear to the wood, trying to see if I could hear anything inside. Silence. I tightened my grip on my beloved dagger, and my other hand grasped the heavy black door handle.

'Wait, what are you doing?' Sylas said, taking a stand in front of the door. I scrunched my face up.

'I'm going in, if that's alright with you. The compass is pointing directly at it, we can't hang around all day?'

Sylas nibbled his lip, looking hesitant. I pushed him aside gently. 'Just because I got injured, doesn't mean I can't look after myself.'

He tutted. 'I know you are more than capable of defending yourself, just at least let me go first. If something is in there, then I am in better shape than you at the moment with your injured arm, so I can take the brunt of it. I can't risk your wounds opening up again, you have lost enough blood.'

I massaged my brow with my thumb and finger, but then gestured for him to go ahead. Sylas drew his sword. The door squealed in complaint as he pulled it open, it probably hadn't been moved in centuries. He took a tentative step in whilst I observed from behind.

The inside was creepy, yet calming. The church looked like it had been untouched by humans for a while, and the wilderness had claimed it as its own. The stained-glass windows cast a pattern of colours along the twig-ridden floor. Large stone archways towered above. Row after row of wooden benches sat, perfectly preserved, all pointing towards the alter.

My eyes fell on an object resting atop the altar. It was a lantern - but not like any I had ever seen before. Small shadows seemed to wreathe around its presence, twisting and curling as if alive. This was something clearly crafted by Fae - could it be used as a weapon though?

'Sylas, look,' I whispered. I needed a closer look, so I slipped past his sturdy frame and marched down the aisle.

'Aurora, wait!' Sylas called. I heard his footsteps behind me, but it was too late - I had placed my hand on the lantern.

At that moment an icy chill swept through me. Like my internal body temperature just dropped to minus degrees. The church fell away around me. It crumpled into... nothingness. White expanse. I swirled around. Sylas was gone. I was alone. The silence felt heavy, surrounding me on all sides. I was in a void where nothing existed but me.

'They are all lying to you.'

The faintest lick of a whisper against my ear. I spun around but there was nobody there. Just white expanse. Then more whispers joined.

'Nothing is as it seems.'

I spun on my heel again. How could I hear these voices when there was nobody here? I kept turning on the spot, disorientated.

A thin, high voice right in my ear. 'You're being betrayed.'

My breath quickened. And then I heard another voice, and this one I recognised all too well. And it sent shivers down my spine.

'Young Aurora. You failed me.' The Queen of Nexonia's steel grey eyes bore into mine as she lounged on her golden throne. A sneer twisted her face. 'You failed me, but you knew the consequences. Bring them in!'

Guards appeared from behind her throne, holding my Ma and Pa hostage with a knife to their necks.

'No!' I cried out. 'Give me just a little longer. I will get your son back for you. Please, I just need a little longer!'

My voice echoed back to me in the void. Like a hundred of me were screaming. I heard the pain in my voice, how it cracked with every emotion. Desperation. My heart slammed against my ribcage. I made to run for my parents, fully prepared to fight the guards who were going to hurt them, but my legs were stuck. I couldn't move an inch. That's when I noticed how light my hand felt, and I stared at it in bewilderment.

'Looking for something?' the Queen chuckled. In her hands she twizzled my dagger.

'Don't!' I begged. 'Please, I'll do anything. Don't harm them, please. *Please.*' I was on my knees. Tears burned at my eyes, but I couldn't tear them from my parents in case it was the last moment I would see them alive.

'You promised to save us, Aurora!' my Ma sobbed. Her beautiful face was blotchy and streaked with tears, and her matching red hair was matted, hanging in clumps around it. I couldn't help her, hug her, save her.

'I tried, Ma, I'm trying. I just need more time,' I begged her. The Queen tilted her head with a wicked smile. I hated her. With every inch of my body. I wanted to kill her now.

The blade of my own dagger glinted as she strolled towards my parents.

'Please, no!' I screamed, my voice so raw and painful as it clawed at my throat. I pounded my fists on the floor but the Queen of Nexonia only ignored me. She raised the dagger - my dagger - above her head, closing her eyes to savour my desperate screams.

'Aurora,' a voice called from somewhere far away. Sylas. It was his voice. 'Aurora, come back to me!'

'Sylas?' I panted, my senses blurring and distorting. The Queens arms were still raised; the dagger pointed directly towards my parents. I felt a tug from afar, like a bond to another world, a feeling that I could leave this nightmare behind if I wanted to.

Again, Sylas called out, 'Aurora, wake up. What's happening? I'm here, I'm here!'

I needed to get out of here before the Queen could hurt my parents. I released myself to the invisible bond that could get me out of here, and the horrific scene before me slipped away. The Queen's face melted away, and then her body, and then my parents, until they all became nothing but a puddle of blood and bones in the whiteness, and suddenly the white was melting too.

I screwed my eyes shut as senses bled together into a cacophony of chaos, and when I opened them, I was back in the church. Breathing hard, my heart pounding wildly, but safe. Sylas's beautiful eyes flicked between mine.

'What happened?' he gasped. Both his hands were on my shoulders as though he had been shaking me.

I tried forming words, but my mouth just gaped. Thoughts scrambled around in my head. 'I- I don't know. The minute I touched that lantern, I just… I wasn't- I wasn't here anymore. The Queen of Nexonia was there; she was about to kill my parents because I failed the mission, and I-' Tears leaked down my cheeks as I recalled the horrors I had just lived through.

'Woah, it's okay. It was just a vision.' Sylas crouched to level with me. He looked me dead in the eyes. 'You just scared me because you went so rigid the second you touched that lantern; I couldn't seem to get through to you. It's like you went to another world entirely.'

'I'm sorry, I-'

'Don't you dare apologise. It's this stupid lantern that did it. You don't think it's the…?'

I nodded, my mouth a tight line. I did indeed think it was the weapon we were looking for. I didn't know how it would work but… it seemed to fit. A lantern crafted by a priest to be kept in a church. And the desire needle had pointed us right to it. But how were we going to use the weapon if we couldn't touch it?

I was getting a hold of my breath now. The pain and doom were fading away and I could think more clearly. 'I think you have to… to fight a vision. When I touched the lantern, I saw the worst scenario I could think of right in front of me, my worst fear. I- I think it's a test or something. But, when you called my name, it grounded me. I knew I could leave the vision before she- before it got to the bad part. I consciously chose to break away from the vision rather than endure it through to the end. I don't think we can take the lantern unless we watch it all the way through.'

Sylas's face sank into his hands.

'I can do it,' I said, trying to stop the wobble in my voice. 'I know what to expect now, I-'

'No,' Sylas said. He angled himself between me and the lantern. 'I know you don't need protecting. Veil knows you are so much stronger than me in every way. But there is no way I'm letting you watch your parents die. I told you before I wished I could take your pain away and that is what I'm going to do.'

He turned and before I could open my mouth to protest, he had clutched the lantern. In an instant, his whole body went rigid. His eyes glazed over, he didn't move, didn't blink. I didn't want Sylas to suffer by having to watch his worst fear play out like I had, but it was too late, he was sucked into the power of the lantern. Only he could draw himself away from that other world.

There was a chance I was wrong. That this wasn't a test, it was simply some cruel vision that served no purpose. But it made sense to be a test. If the vision was meant to trap us forever, there wouldn't have been an option to opt out. And although I hated the thought of Sylas having to live out his worst fear, I was secretly flooded with relief that I wouldn't have to watch the two people I loved most in this life die before me. Real or not - that would have haunted me forever. And Sylas had ensured I didn't have to live through that.

His hand was trembling as I gathered it in my own. I studied his face. His mouth moved to make words not heard in this dimension, his eyes were so filled with terror, with horror. A small tear slipped down his cheek. My heart ached just watching him as he battled through the mental nightmares.

I got on my tiptoes and whispered to him, 'I'm here. I'm right here.'

His hand ever so slightly tightened around mine. It felt like the longest wait of my life. I stood there, observing every minute change on his face as he rode the waves of pain, anger, dread, just like I had.

And then he took a huge gasp as another large tear ran down his face. He let go of my hand, backing away into a pew.

'It's alright, it's alright, it's just me,' I said, holding up both palms.

His eyes adjusted back to the setting of the church, the situation we were in. He put a hand to his eye, realising it was damp in the real world too, and brushed the tears away hastily. I wondered what his vision had been about - what was *his* worst fear?

He cleared his throat, straightening up. 'I did it. I watched it to the end. We should be able to get the lantern now.'

He made to move towards it, but I stopped him with a hand to the chest. I found myself more concerned with if he was alright, rather than seeing if we had been successful with the lantern right now. I reached for his hand; it was like a block of ice. 'Are you okay?'

He looked down at my hand for a moment before taking it away and mumbling, 'Yes, fine.'

I pushed away the hurt that stabbed in my chest. It was the first time I had been so openly tender towards anyone but my parents in years and it had been shunned away. I cursed my traitorous heart for feeling anything at all towards him. I couldn't be weak. Not with so much at stake.

He approached the lantern again, warily clasping the handle, and this time he wasn't transported into a horrific vision. It was beautiful; a glass dome encased in swirling patterns of sturdy gold metal, with small, playful shadows wafting from within. So how could this lantern serve as a weapon? Perhaps, when ignited, it could blind an opponent, or maybe it could unleash a burst of searing light to burn them?

But when I took the lantern from Sylas to examine it more closely, my heart sank. There was no way to light it - no apparent mechanism to pry open the glass and ignite the wick inside.

'I don't understand,' I said, my eyebrows knitting together. 'We have come all this way for this "weapon", and we can't even use it? The desire needle directed us *here*, but maybe this isn't it, perhaps we missed something?'

Sylas shrugged half-heartedly; the ghost of horror still lining his face. We looked around the church, in every dusty corner and crevice, under pews, behind moth-eaten curtains. But there was nothing else. No gleaming sword or magic staff. I couldn't help but feel deflated, we had come all this way for a weapon to defeat the Shadow Warden, which had turned out to be a lantern that didn't even seem to work. Was the Fae Queen just setting us up for failure, finding it funny to torment us along the way? I thought of those words echoing around my head once again: *They are all lying to you. You're being betrayed.*

Lumen was waiting for us faithfully outside, with a dead squirrel hanging from her mouth. She offered it to me and despite the situation, I couldn't help but smile.

'I'm all good, Lumen. It's all yours.' I found my eyes wondering to Sylas, to see that familiar smirk upon his face, but he was solemn as he mounted Lumen. I felt my own smile slide away.

* * *

It was my job to look after the pack with our supplies, and Sylas's to look after the lantern. We had travelled to the nearest forest in order to get the cover of trees for the night and recover. I stripped off more fabric from my cloak, which was growing shorter by the day, and unwound the blood-red bandage I currently wore. I cringed at the wounds. Whilst they were healing well, it made me queasy to look at the mangled flesh for too long. It would most likely leave a permeant scar so that I may never forget the trauma I had endured. I doused the wounds with some fresh water before attempting to bandage my arm up with the new fabric.

Sylas had barely spoken all day, but as I struggled to wrap the fabric one-handed, he shuffled toward me.

'Let me,' he said softly. I watched him as he worked, his tongue between his teeth as he wound the fabric around my arm, tying it in a neat knot to keep it in place.

'Thank you,' I said. He blew the hair from his eyes and the green-brown were upon my own. He managed a small smile for me and nodded his head before sinking back into his quietness, slumped against the tree. I wanted to ask him about the vision he had, whatever was so obviously haunting him, but it felt too vulnerable, too personal. I wasn't sure he would want to talk about it. Not to me.

Perhaps if we got some rest, he would feel better in the morning. In the light of a fresh day.

'I'm going to get some rest. Goodnight, Sylas,' I said with a smile.

'Goodnight, Aurora.'

I turned onto my side, shuffling around until I felt comfortable. I fell asleep soundly that night, exhausted from the past few weeks. Yet when I awoke, it was still night, a speckled blanket of stars overhead. I shifted over to my other side and spotted Sylas, still sitting with his knees drawn to his chest - the exact same position he'd been in when I fell asleep. I propped myself up on my elbows.

'Sylas,' I called gently, breaking his distant stare. He looked over and smiled gently. 'Is everything okay?'

'Yeah, everything's fine, you can go back to sleep. We still have a few more hours until dawn.'

'What about you? Why aren't you sleeping?'

He looked away then. Even in the darkness I could see a flush of colour on his cheeks.

'Truthfully, I don't really sleep at night. At least, not since we started this journey.'

I sat up. 'But why? You need rest?'

'Yes, but I didn't feel right sleeping at night, leaving you and Lumen unprotected. There are bad things out here, and it's never truly safe. So, I like to keep watch.'

I blinked. 'But how have you been staying awake all day if you don't sleep?'

'Sometimes when it gets closer to dawn, I try and rest for a little while. Mostly, I take short naps on Lumen's back,' he admitted.

I stared at him, not sure what to say. All this time, he hadn't been sleeping, staying alert all night in case of danger. Meanwhile, I'd been sleeping peacefully, completely unaware of the lengths he had gone to protect Lumen and I from the very start. Being an assassin had made me fast and sharp, skilled at combat and deadly with my aim. But at the end of the day, I'd always been able to come home and sleep soundly in my own bed. I hadn't even considered that it wasn't safe to let my guard down when we slept out under the stars. This wasn't Nexonia; this was the Untamed - the place where all sorts of beasts and creatures prowled the land, day and night.

'I really appreciate that, Sylas. But from now, we'll take turns. You're right; we should have someone on guard at night. I've had my rest, so now it's time for yours,' I said resolutely, sitting bolt straight and removing my dagger from my boot to emphasise my point.

But he was shaking his head, 'No, it's okay. I don't mind watching over you both, making sure everyone's safe.'

'Well, that doesn't matter. We can take it in turns from now. I cannot believe you have been doing this, and sleeping on Lumen's back for a few minutes a day is hardly sustainable. I'm surprised you haven't fallen off!'

He chuckled, 'I've come close. A few times, I jerked awake just before I toppled over.'

I was chuckling now, thinking back. 'I always wondered why you were so quiet back there. Sylas, you really didn't need to do that. I would have been happy to take turns at night. That's what we will do from now. It's your turn to rest.'

'No, I couldn't-'

'Stop being so gentlemanly and just go to sleep. Make the most of the time we have left until dawn.'

He stared at me for a beat. I held my breath, taking in every inch of his strong features, that devastating smile. Finally, he shrugged and sighed.

'So stubborn. Fine. I'll get some sleep. But wake me up if you need me for anything.'

'Yes, yes. Goodnight.'

'Goodnight again, Aurora.'

And I watched him for the rest of the night, shaking my head in disbelief that he had stayed awake all this time - for us, for me.

Chapter Fourteen

We had been travelling for the past few days with nothing but fields and fresh air for company when I saw smoke rising in the distance - great plumes of ashy grey disrupting the otherwise black inkiness of the night. There was a large hill just east of our path, and we decided to head that way to get a good vantage point. The climb was steep, and as we neared the top, I caught the faint crackling of a fire in the distance.

When we finally reached the summit, we surveyed the scene sprawling below - and it was not what I'd expected. A village, much larger than the first one we had visited, lay nestled in the valley, with a massive, roaring bonfire at its centre. Around the fire, little shadow figures hurried about like ants.

I inhaled deeply as the smell of roasting meat hit me, and my eyes found the hog roast, spinning slowly over the flames, loaded with pigs so large they didn't seem real. My mouth watered. Food. Shelter. A bed. My body yearned for all of it. It had been weeks since I'd eaten anything other than Fae bread or the same kind of meat that we had managed to capture in our traps.

Sylas caught my eye and we both nodded. A silent agreement we would stay here for the night. Lumen didn't need to be told; she marched towards the village with speed. Perhaps she smelt the meat too.

The walls surrounding the village got larger and more intimidating the closer we drew. Thick, barred gates loomed and I couldn't help but think how pathetic the first village defences were compared to these. But I knew it was necessary; everyone knew the further north you went, the worse the creatures lurking in the Untamed became. My craving for comfort and food was gnawed at by a sudden uncertainty.

'Are we sure this is a good idea?' Sylas murmured, voicing my own concerns.

I swallowed. The truth was - I wasn't sure. My gut fluttered uneasily as I stared up at the wall, something about this village felt unsettling and I couldn't put my finger on why. But my body was yearning for a real bed, some food other than rabbit or squirrel, the safety of strong walls. I wanted it so badly. And we were so close, it was all just on the other side of these gates. I could smell the sizzling pork, rich and savoury. My mouth was filled with saliva as I nodded. Sylas took the pack from me and stuffed the lantern inside.

When we got to the gates, we found that there was no guard, it appeared the entire village was taking part in the bonfire we had witnessed from the hill. I called out for someone, but it seems they were all pre-occupied with the fire to notice. I gave the gates a rattle, but they were locked, of course. Disappointment hit me. I had got too excited with the prospect of having a proper meal and sleeping on a real bed, to be met with a locked gate.

Just as I was about to turn away, a figure emerged from a nearby wooden house.

'Excuse me,' I called through the bars. 'Is there a place for two travellers and a horse to settle for the night? Please.'

The small figure turned. Her dark cloak draped over her slight frame and a hood cast her face into deep shadow. As she approached, the flickering torchlight flanking the gate illuminated her features, and I bit my lip to stifle a gasp. Beneath the hood, where a face should have been, was a mask of wood and bone, unmistakably carved into the visage of a ghoul - hollowed eyes and a gaping mouth. Behind the mask, her eyes darted between us. She paused briefly before unlocking the gates, the clink of iron bracelets on her slender arms the only sound breaking the silence. Without a word, she pushed the gate open just enough for us to slip through.

'Thank you,' I said, but the woman did not say a word.

Lumen snickered uneasily. We walked slowly to the heart of the village, every muscle in my body was alert. The air grew thicker with the scents of incense, rosemary and sage - and an undercurrent of excitement. More people with masks hurried by, and I realised each mask resembled a different creature or beast that must live in the Untamed.

They scurried toward the bonfire like moths to a flame, laying clumps of herbs, woven charms, animal skulls, twigs and feathers, before the great flames. Some were drawing symbols on each other's arms or backs with pastes of ash, chalk, and water. We had clearly arrived right before something was about to happen, on a very important night.

I scanned the chaos and spotted an older woman sitting on a stool a little distance from the main action. Her grey hair poked out the back of a mask.

'Sorry to bother you,' I said as I approached. 'What is happening here?'

She turned to me, and to my relief she pulled off the mask to reveal a friendly, aged face and gummy smile.

'I don't recognise either of you, you newcomers?' she asked warmly. I nodded, feeding her a lie about us coming from another village.

She nodded knowingly. 'I see, don't get many newcomers here. Usually people leaving rather than coming.' She leaned in confidentially. 'Going down south, of course. Less trouble down there.'

I didn't know if I agreed with that, so far it seemed like no matter where we were in the Untamed Territory, chaos would find you.

'You're lucky, you have arrived on a very special night. We are performing our spiritual cleansing,' she explained. 'Once a fortnight we like to honour the spirits and creatures that roam this land by offering gifts and treasures while we cleanse our space.'

Sylas scoffed. 'You want to *honour* the creatures out there?'

I gave him a hard nudge in the ribs, but the woman only nodded fervently.

'Why, yes, of course! We can try and fight what's out there, but they're much more powerful than we are. We believe the best way to co-exist alongside them is to create harmony. We perform these rituals to show we respect them, we bow down to them, and in return they leave us alone - for the most part. We are only just getting started, go join in. We haven't had guests in forever!'

'Oh, we don't want to intrude,' I said quickly. 'We just hoped to find some lodgings for the night and a stable for our horse.' I gestured to Lumen, who was once again glamoured, her usual radiance dimmed.

The woman flapped a hand dismissively. 'Oh, my sister has some spare rooms you can use for the night. And we have stables, just there - you see?' She pointed through the smoky haze and, sure enough, beyond the silhouettes of people weaving around the fire, I glimpsed a large stable barn. 'I'll take your horse over and then go and find my sister. You kids go and have fun - join in! I'll find you once I have spoken to my sister.'

She got to her feet and took Lumen's reins, gesturing for us to join the crowd. Lumen cast a nervous look over her shoulder as she was led away, and I felt a pang of guilt at parting with her. We moved toward the gathering, and soon someone was shoving masks into our hands. Mine had a gaping mouth and horrifically arched eyebrows - I was told it resembled a Banshee - and Sylas's was structured with bone, complete with antlers branching from each side - a Wendigo, we were told. I couldn't help but shiver as I stared at the masks, thinking about what it would be like to run into either of these creatures on our journey.

I slipped the mask over my face. Sylas stared down uneasily at his, but I nodded at him to put his on too. It felt much too risky to refuse participation on a night that was so sacred to these people. We were then ushered to join a ring of villagers around the fire, watching as more masked figures danced before the flames. As they moved, they chanted, their voices low and hypnotic, reverberating through my chest. They moved slowly and in perfect synch with one another, their gestures seemed to mimic different creatures - sometimes with a heavy, hulking presence, sometimes with light, airy steps that evoked delicate spirits. The fire's glow cast rippling light over their faces, distorting their eyes under the mask with its flickering heat.

Then sounded the constant beat of hands on drums, and everyone bent their knees, clapping to the rhythm against their thighs. Sylas and I stuck out like a sore thumb, the only ones that weren't following along, and so I sank into a squat and attempted to match the beat, nudging Sylas to do the same. I could see him doing his best to copy, but when his eyes caught mine as a woman began to sing in a warbled tune, we both had to look away and bite our lips to stop the bark of laughter from escaping.

We had to endure a good half an hour or so of the lady's screeching, and when it finally ended, a man stumbled forward. He was clearly an elder, his wrinkled skin seemed to hang off his very skeleton.

He cleared his throat, and from the immediate silence that fell, I could tell he was an important figure. His voice had not deteriorated from age as he called out loudly, 'Good evening all, we gather for the Night of Spirits, dedicated to those much more powerful, much more supernatural than ourselves. We gather to worship you, creatures and spirits of the Untamed, and to seek forgiveness for occupying your land, and in exchange for peace, we offer ourselves to you tonight. We will never harm you, and we ask for your mercy in return. We are grateful for your presence, for the honour of living among you, and we bow to your power.'

He lifted his voice upwards, towards the stars and the sky, 'We dance now, to show our union to your almighty forces.'

And everyone did so. Every villager stripped off their masks and cast them aside, revealing thankfully normal-looking faces underneath, and this time, when the drums started again, they were fast and joyful. People came together, either in groups or as couples, and started to dance and twirl around one another. The vibe had completely shifted in a matter of moments. The shadows seemed to lift as laughter and chatter broke out as the people whirled around the flames. Skirts billowed in swirling blurs, couples spinning and swaying, while children wove between them, stomping to the beat. It was a beautiful sight. As I watched, a smile crept onto my face. Despite the lurking dangers beyond these walls, they seemed so happy, so carefree.

Whilst it was wonderful watching everyone have fun, I wondered if it would be sensible for Sylas and I to try and track down the old woman's sister who had lodging for us so that we could rest. But as I turned to voice this to Sylas, I found his hand outstretched to me. I looked down at it, observing every callous, every scar on his hand. There was a small, nervous smile on his face, his eyes sparked with daring.

'Would you care to join me for a dance, Aurora?' he asked softly, watching me with those mesmerising eyes. I think my heart stopped beating for a second. I hadn't felt that way since... since Cain. I knew I shouldn't - the way he made my heart flutter was a feeling I had forbidden myself from ever letting anyone make me feel again. But it was only one dance, right?

I gave him my hand.

His fingers curled around mine, fitting into the grooves of my knuckles. The pace was fast, and at first, we whipped our heads around, shaking our bodies loose, laughter spilling from our throats. He spun me, watching with dimpled cheeks, fascinated by my every movement. I liked his eyes on me, the way they took me in. Like they saw me. *All* of me.

I had never been much of a dancer, but I moved surprisingly easily, letting the drums and the beat take over, guiding my hips and swaying with the rhythm. For just a moment, I felt at ease. Free, almost. Shaking away the tension my body had been storing up. The weight of my burdens was still there, and my heart still ached for my parents, but right now, all I could focus on was *him*, standing before me.

The music began to slow, and soon the couples moved at a gentle pace, clutching one another as the drum beat softened. Sylas's hand hovered over the small of my back, unsure. I nodded with a shy smile to show that it was okay, and his hand settled there. It felt like it belonged. He pulled me in ever so slightly and I wrapped my hands around his neck like the other couples had done. We swayed slowly - two becoming one. Locked together.

His eyes were fixed intently on my face, and I found myself unable to look away. The excitement and comfort I felt meeting his gaze was addictive. I couldn't decide which eye to focus on - the dark, calming depths of brown or the vibrant sparks of green. My gaze kept shifting between them as I fought to keep from glancing at his mouth.

As a dark brown curl found its way across his eye, he didn't move his hand from my back to brush it away. Without thinking I pushed it aside. My mouth fell open as I realised how brazen I had been, but he only chuckled gently at the expression on my face. Such a warm smile. A boy who had clearly been through horrors I couldn't imagine. And he was smiling at me.

'Penny for your thoughts?' I said. He gave me a mock frown.

'I don't think so. I don't want a penny launched at my face again.'

I shook my head; I couldn't stop *smiling*. 'I promise nothing will fly at your face. Go on, tell me.'

His eyes flicked over my face. 'I am thinking... that whilst I am excited to get your parents back for you... I will miss this. You. It has been nice getting to know you, Aurora.'

The words burned a hole right through my chest and I bit the inside of my cheek. Once this mission was done, we would go our separate ways. He would go back to being the Queen's guard and I suppose I was meant to go back to being the Queen's assassin. Although I most definitely wouldn't work for her anymore if I could help it.

And I was so excited to get my parents back. I missed them more than anything in the world. But I realised I would also miss Sylas too. His company. His smile. And I hadn't admitted that to myself until now.

'Your turn,' Sylas said, dipping his head to catch the eyes that had wondered to his chest as my thoughts spiralled. I was silent for a while as I looked up at him.

'I'm thinking I will miss you too. What the Queen has done, threatening my family, was the worst thing that has ever happened to me. But at least I met you. The one good thing that came from it.'

His eyes sparkled and his hands brought me in a little. He was so *close*. His breath was soft against my lips. His eyes so devastating up close, full of mischief and intelligence. He was inches away from my lips, if he just inclined his head ever so slightly...

The drums stopped, and everyone around us broke apart. The elder stepped forward and silence fell again. I reluctantly dropped my arms from Sylas's neck and we broke apart as everyone backed away from the fire, watching the elder as he prowled forward.

'It is time we move onto the final and most important part of the Night of Spirits. It is time for our big sacrifice to show the Untamed creatures that we are true to our word. Of course, we always select one of our own for this sacrifice. But tonight, we are spared of this duty, for tonight I have been informed that we are joined by not one, but *two* newcomers. I have deemed them a most perfect sacrifice for tonight. Seize them!' His gnarled finger unfurled and landed on us. My heart froze. My mind froze. Everything happened in slow motion.

The air exploded with shouts. In seconds my hands had been pinned to my back. My mind hadn't even processed the words quick enough for me to react.

'Get off her!' Sylas yelled, his voice raw against his throat. He reached out to me but was shoved back by a huge, beefy man. Sylas swung at him, landing an impressive blow to the man's jaw. The man fell to the floor, but in a matter of moments Sylas had been swallowed up by a crowd of several other bodies, also pinning his hands behind his back and binding them with rope. I screamed and thrashed wildly but it was all in vain. Sylas and I were both wicked fighters, but we were up against a whole village of people who were drunk on camaraderie and the power of the ritual.

I was surrounded on all sides, faces looming in and out of my vision, shouting and screaming as I was hauled up a set of wooden steps onto a platform before the fire. A long pole stood at the centre of the platform, and a man twice my size bound my wrists to it, the rough rope biting into my skin. Behind me, I heard Sylas's angry protests and felt him being wrenched into place, tied back-to-back with me against the same post. We both struggled against the restraints, but the villagers only hissed and screeched louder. The flames below cast twisted shadows, their flickering light making the villagers even more terrifying without their masks.

This was my fault. I had let the hunger in my belly drive me here, to a place so obviously unsafe.

'I'm sorry, Sylas,' I said, my voice cracking on his name.

Tears spilt from my eyes, carving their way down my cheeks. I was so angry at myself. At the world. For throwing challenge after challenge at us. Mostly, I was just so tired. Of the constant running and fighting and being on guard. Back home, even as an assassin, I'd been able to let my guard down at night, to leave that darker part of me behind when I was with my parents. To just relax without having to watch my back. But here, I'd had no such refuge. Being alert all day, for weeks on end, had drained me and made me lazy. Made me make this vital mistake. I felt the fight leave my body as my head slumped.

'Aurora, it's okay, it's okay. This isn't your fault. We didn't know these people were *psychos*.' He spat that last word.

I felt his hand find mine. My heart burned for him. Burned to turn to him and just sink into his arms and sob, but I couldn't. I was bound to the stupid pole. The elder parted his way through the crowd.

I swear by the Veil my heart stopped beating when I beheld what he had in his hands.

A giant cleaver. The reflection of the fire glistened against that huge blade. Every part of me pounded in pure horror. The elder took his time, moving slowly as the crowd cheered him on - relieved that they had been spared the role of potentially becoming a sacrifice for another fortnight. His eyes locked onto us, cold and unyielding, filled with the merciless resolve of a leader who could show no weakness in front of his people. Or perhaps he had none at all.

He climbed the steps and approached us, at the last minute turning to the crowd to bellow, 'We will recite our saying and make our sacrifice. Everyone!'

The villagers merged into a single, terrifying mass as they chanted in monotone unison; 'We gather tonight to give ourselves to you, to make the biggest sacrifice we can make in this land - our own bodies and souls. In exchange, all we ask for is peace.'

And then the elder turned to us.

'Please,' Sylas begged. The pain in his voice made my chest constrict. 'Take my life, not hers. You don't need two sacrifices!'

The elder shook his head, 'Two sacrifices are stronger than one. You will both die tonight.'

Sylas kept pleading. He was choking on his words. My heart felt like it wasn't beating anymore, the world was swallowed away - Sylas would have sacrificed himself, for *me*? He cared for me *that* much. I meant *that* much to him.

But the elder seemed to sense this, and therefore turned to me first. He raised that huge blade, a thin slice of metal above my head, aiming it to cleave my skull in two. Sylas was screaming and struggling against the bonds. The pole shook violently but held firm. Sylas let out a cry, so guttural, so heart-felt, that every inch of my heart hurt for him. Even the crowd had stopped chanting at that sound of raw, unbearable pain.

I closed my eyes. I had taken a lot of lives on behalf of the Queen. I had done many things wrong. I had many regrets. But meeting Sylas was one thing I had needed in my life. To show me that love was still possible for me.

Love.

Chapter Fifteen

A singular shout sounded out. Then another. And another. I opened my eyes.

The blade was just inches away.

Sweat poured down my face, the salty drops stinging my eyes as I turned to the crowd. Something was stirring amongst them; people were being knocked about, stumbling backward.

'Lumen!' I shrieked as I spotted her midnight-black head through the masses. She was kicking and bucking her way through the crowd, her glamour gone. Her long, proud legs stretched out, peppering jaw-breaking kicks to anyone who stood in her way. The crowd parted before her, people jumping back and dragging their children away from the wild, beautiful beast.

The elder's hands seemed frozen in time, the blade glinting above me as he watched Lumen. He was transfixed. And she was magnificent. She must have kicked the stable door down to get to us when she heard Sylas's shouting.

'Quick,' Sylas whispered while everyone's attention was on Lumen. 'Bend your leg upwards and rest your foot on my knee.' I did as he instructed, balancing on one leg as I carefully placed my foot where he indicated. I felt his fingers grasp the inside of my boot as he retracted my dagger. With one hand, he awkwardly sawed at the bonds holding his wrists. There was a soft thud as his bindings hit the wooden platform. Without turning, he began cutting my bonds. My hands were free.

My ropes hit the ground, and this time the elder heard the noise and turned to me. I watched his face grow furious - and my boot swung right into his wrinkled old groin. He doubled over, and I dodged just in time. I felt a cold woosh of wind as the blade severed the air where I had been only a heartbeat ago, and plastered into the wooden pole. The swing would have carved my head in.

Sylas grabbed the elder by his shirt and picked him up with a singular hand - so fuelled with anger, he was shaking from head to toe. And with incredible strength, he hauled the elder straight into the fire. People gasped as the embers flared and the fire roared at its new fuel. Screams pierced the night, but above them all, Sylas's voice rang louder: 'There's your damn sacrifice!'

And then we were running. Everything blurred - houses, people, fire - it all bled into one. I swooped down to pick the pack off the floor from where it had been abandoned. My muscles screamed, but I didn't stop. I was groaning and crying uncontrollably as we ran, Lumen's hoofbeats pounding behind us. Shouts echoed after us; they were coming for us - and they were angry.

'Get to the gate!' someone yelled. Figures closed in from all sides, but I didn't look at them; my focus was locked on the gate ahead. I heard Sylas's heavy breath beside me.

Suddenly, someone stepped into our path, hands braced, but neither Sylas nor I stopped. We each took a side and delivered a powerful gut-punch, and the man keeled over as we barrelled past. We got to the gate, our breaths scraping against our throats, and Sylas scrambled with the lock. I felt violently sick, but this wasn't the time. Thudding footsteps were growing louder, they would be onto us in seconds. The lock finally clicked, and he yanked the gates open, ushering me through before following.

I sprinted for my life. My legs moved of their own accord, carrying me away from the mess we had created. I noticed the shouts and screams fading behind us. They weren't following us. Veil above!

We had got away.

I dared a glance back and stumbled to a stop.

'No!' I howled. Lumen was rearing and bucking, for the villagers had looped a rope around her neck. 'Don't touch her!'

I made to run for her, but Sylas caught me around the waist. I struggled against him, beating at his hands. 'Get *off*, we have to get her. They will kill her!'

It was unbearable watching her thrash and whinny in the swarm as they dragged her back inside the gates.

'We can't, Aurora!' Sylas shouted. 'We can't go back for her right now. They will kill us too.'

'We need to fight for her, they will hurt her,' I cried, still pounding my fists. 'I will slash their throats. Every single one of them!'

But he wouldn't let me go. They closed the gates, and Lumen was dragged out of sight. Sylas slowly released his hands and I stood for a moment, watching in disbelief, before falling to my knees. Exhausted sobs wracked my body as I laid my forehead to the cold, muddy floor. Sylas sat down next to me, and waited as I sobbed all my frustrations into the earth.

All I wanted was to save my parents. Was that so hard? Why did *everything* have to go so wrong?

After what felt like hours of staring at the closed gates, Sylas gently helped me to my feet. I felt numb. I couldn't think straight anymore. This was all too much. I just let him pull me up, he took my hand and led me away. It felt as though I was leaving a piece of my heart behind. We walked for a while until we were a safe distance away and he found a good place for us to sleep for the night. Sylas guided me to sit down and allowed me to slump against him for comfort.

Before sleep claimed me, I murmured against his chest, 'You better wake me up when it's my turn to keep watch. We are taking it in turns from now, remember.'

'Of course, Aurora.'

He didn't wake me, obviously.

Chapter Sixteen

We trudged on without Lumen. I had been determined to storm the village and reclaim her, but Sylas assured me that doing so would result in instant death for all of us. Our progress felt sluggish without her long, Fae legs which had covered hundreds of miles with ease. I knew Lumen had been bound to stay with us, being assigned by the Fae, but her loyalty went beyond that. She had been so excited to see us after we escaped the Nautlian's, had dragged my body to safety, had saved us from becoming the village sacrifice. She had become such an important part of this journey.

And now she was gone.

Anger seethed in my heart whenever I pictured those villagers dragging her away.

Sylas noticed my curled fists and nudged me gently. 'Hey, you alright?'

We were sitting under a wide oak tree and eating the last of the Fae bread. I fixed him with a stare, and he exhaled, knowing it was a stupid question.

'I'm sorry,' I said, bowing my head. 'It's not you I'm mad at, obviously. I just feel so frustrated. She saved us, Sylas.'

'I know she did. And trust me, we will get her back. I promise,' he said firmly.

I gave him a weak smile for his efforts at cheering me up. I fumbled in the pack to check the Desire Compass and ensure we were headed in the right direction still. My jaw dropped and I shuffled round to show Sylas.

'Look, the desire needle is going crazy. I think we are getting close!' The needle was twitching rapidly at a point located between north and north-east. Sylas dusted his hands and got to his feet, giving me a hand up.

For the past few days, the desire needle had flicked between leading us on to find the Divinal Stone, and going back for Lumen, so I closed my eyes and concentrated wholly on the Stone. Imagining the feeling of clutching the Stone in my hand. When I opened my eyes again, the desire needle was dead straight. We followed its direction deeper into the forest, stumbling over thick roots that upturned the ground. Tall spindly trees blocked out the light ahead. Our surroundings began to fall eerily quiet, the normal sounds of the world choked away by the thickening undergrowth. There only seemed to be a gentle hushing of the wind, whispering to the leaves.

'Sylas, look.' I had stopped in my tracks and pointed towards a thick curtain of vines. I wouldn't have noticed what they concealed if a gentle breeze hadn't hit them at just the right moment, and they billowed backwards to reveal a hollow cave entrance embedded into a moss-covered mound. I felt something, deep in my very bones, a subtle hum of power calling to me from within. Sylas must have felt it too, for he nodded.

'I think the Stone's inside. The compass is pointing straight at it.' I shifted the pack higher on my shoulders and drew out my dagger, the one that had had saved my life so many times. Sylas unsheathed his sword, and we approached slowly, every tread careful, every snapping twig making us suck in a breath. My heart thumped wildly.

We had come all this way, fought so many creatures and escaped by the skin of our teeth too many times to count, all to get the Divinal Stone.

And now we were here.

The lantern was safe in my pack, I would pull it out when I needed it - not that I knew *how* it would help us - but for now I needed my hands free.

Sylas used his sword to draw back the vines. I cringed, almost expecting something to leap out of the cave's dark mouth. But there was only stillness and silence.

'Maybe I should go in and scope things out?' Sylas whispered. I shook my head firmly.

'I'm coming with you.'

He smiled at my stubbornness before his face solidified again. Hard and serious. He entered into the cave first and I followed in behind him, letting the veil of vines fall behind us like a solid sheet. The tiny streams of light filtering into the cave now faltered completely. We were submerged into total darkness. A steady drip of water from somewhere deep within the cave was the only indication that it stretched onwards, otherwise we were walking in blind.

But I could *feel* that ever-increasing strum of power. And if a mere human could feel the presence of the Stone, I could only imagine how powerful it was for the Fae. Queen Velraxis had spoken about the Stone's abilities to magnify the power of Fae who possessed it, or even those who were in its presence. As if the magic rubbed off on them.

The darkness was imposing, I physically felt its weight settle onto my shoulders. This must be what the lantern was for - to help us see the Shadow Warden in this otherwise impenetrable darkness. Shoving my dagger into my waistband, I extracted the lantern from the pack eagerly and held it up in the gloom. I could barely see it even though it was just inches from my face. Nothing happened. It didn't produce even a flicker of light. I heard Sylas's disappointed sigh echo off the walls.

'Perhaps we have to go in further for it to work?' I suggested, even though every thought in my head was screaming at me to turn around and run.

The air hung heavy with a foreboding that reminded me of the dread I'd felt when approaching the Fae Land. Sylas reached for my hand in the darkness and held it tightly. With his other hand, sword still in his grip, he pressed the flat of his knuckles against the wall to feel the route ahead. I mirrored his movements, letting my knuckles brush against the rough, damp stone as we carefully navigated the cave's twists and turns.

We edged forward slowly. It was so cold in here; I couldn't stop shivering, even under my thick cloak. The lantern stayed unlit. Useless.

It seemed we were descending into nothingness - darkness itself. Only the slow dripping water guided us further and further in. What if we walked forever? What if this cave was some kind of illusion with no end?

But as soon as those thoughts started to spiral - I felt it again. The thread

118

of power. Tugging me closer.

The Divinal Stone.

'I can feel it, Sylas. I think we need to go a little further.'

Sylas murmured his agreement. We kept shuffling forwards, knuckles still pressed against the wall to guide us.

Then slowly, steadily, a blue light in the distance began to grow clearer. At first just a tiny pin-prick, but it grew brighter as we approached. We eventually stepped over some stony rubble and into a circular space within the cave. I stared around in awe. Bioluminescent glow worms covered the entire ceiling of the cave, bathing the space in an otherworldly light, like clusters of brilliant blue stars. Their shimmering glow reflected in the small pools scattered across the cave floor, giving the place an enchanted feel. Jagged stacks of rock jutted down from above, their edges so sharp they looked as though they could slice you in half without effort. And the feeling in here was strong.

Power.

I could almost smell it, touch it. But then where was it?

I looked over to Sylas who gave a nod. We reluctantly broke apart and began searching every corner, every nook, every crevice of the place. It was in here, I knew it.

But we returned to the middle of the space minutes later, both empty handed.

'I don't understand,' I said, running a hand over my face. 'It has to be here. I can *feel* it so strongly, calling to me, but I just can't place its exact location.'

We had gone from the very start of the cave to here. There was not a singular spot we had missed. There were no other entrances to other tunnels that we could have gone down. I tilted my head and searched the depths of the glow above, trying to see if the Divinal Stone might have been embedded into the roof, but found nothing. Random pebbles littered the ground, and I was hit with an uncomfortable thought.

'What if one of these pebbles is the Divinal Stone? What if part of the challenge is trying to figure out which one it is?' I picked one up, turning it over in my hands to see if I could find a special marking or symbol on its flat face. All this time I had assumed the Divinal Stone would be instantly recognisable, but perhaps I was wrong. Maybe that would make things too easy.

Sylas shook his head.

I let the pebble clatter to the ground. 'I would love to see your great idea then.'

He knelt to the ground before one of the shallow pools. His face reflected back up at him, brows crinkled in thought.

'I think it's in one of these-' He reached out a finger lightly over the water but snatched it back as I cried out.

'Don't be stupid! You can't put your hand in there. Next thing you know something will grab you like it did to me at the lake!'

He blinked. 'It's a lot shallower than the lake, Aurora.'

I crossed my arms and huffed. 'Well, you don't know, there might be... poisonous shrimp or- or something in there,' I said, letting my sentence trail off.

Despite the circumstances, a slow grin spread on Sylas's face. 'Poisonous... *shrimp?*'

'Or something of the sort, yes. Look, just wait.' I returned to the rubble near the entrance of the circular chamber, setting down the lantern as I rummaged through the rocks until I found a sturdy stick. Bringing it over to where Sylas knelt by the pool, I crouched beside him and carefully lowered the stick into the water. It found the bottom of the pool about half of an arm's length down. I twirled the stick around the depths, trying to feel if there was anything stone-shaped. Nothing.

I shuffled over to the next pool and repeated the process of jabbing the stick in and feeling around. Once again, I felt nothing, but some foreign glowing insect scuttled out the water, making me recoil. I moved to each pool in turn, waiting for the stick to connect with something.

And then it did. It wasn't stone-shaped, but it was small and solid. I rolled up my sleeve, but Sylas gently pushed me aside and reached in himself. He extracted his arm from the water, revealing a small titanium box that fit snugly in his palm. He turned it over; it was completely sealed. The thrumming of power felt even stronger than ever.

'Try and open it,' I breathed. Sylas tried prising the box open, but it was stead-fast. He shook it slightly. Our eyes widened as something rattled inside. 'That's the Stone.'

My heart was hammering so fast I thought it might burst.

'We need to go somewhere, somewhere I can try and smash the box open,' Sylas said, getting to his feet. He was right, although it seemed that we were alone in the cave, it was so quiet here that the thought of trying to smash open the box made me cringe. I nodded in agreement, and we hopped over pools to make our way to the exit.

'Even if we can't get it open, I'm sure Queen Velraxis could use her powers to unlock it?' I suggested hopefully.

That's when I felt the whole cave shudder. The ground trembled. Rocks skittered along the floor and the pools of water rippled violently. Something was stirring.

The Shadow Warden was here.

Chapter Seventeen

I could feel my pulse in my eyeballs. I stumbled, trying to keep my balance as the ground increased its shaking. The very walls of the cave were quivering now too, and I was extremely wary of the stacks of rock that hung above us like poised daggers. There came a dull thudding from Sylas's hand - the Stone was slamming against the metal box. I could almost hear it whispering in excitement. I snatched the box from him and shoved it into my pocket, drawing my dagger from my waistband.

We both watched the entrance to the space, waiting as the rumbling grew louder and a fresh wind whipped around the cave. My hair was blown into a frenzy, strands ripped free from my plait and billowed around me. Every muscle, every cell, every fibre of my being was taut in suspense as we waited for the Shadow Warden to emerge from the dark tunnel ahead.

But then it all stopped. Everything went still.

Our heavy breaths were the only sound now. The bioluminescent glow worms on the walls flickered, casting eerie shadows that danced in the corners of my vision. A slow scraping sound echoed down the hallway. Something was shifting. It was as if the very foundations of the cave were changing.

'Sylas,' I breathed, as thin cracks began to separate the ground beneath our feet. The stone was dividing, splintering into thousands of thunder bolt cracks.

A disgusting sucking sound echoed through the cave. My gaze snapped toward the noise, and I watched in horror as shadows, creeping from every corner and crevice of the cave, began to move. They slithered toward one another, swirling into a thick, writhing mass that merged and congealed. In the heart of the darkness, something was beginning to take form - something *physical*. The shadows were climbing each other, shaping themselves into a towering figure, and finally solidifying into a massive black hand.

More shadows curled from the hand as it stretched and flexed its fingers.

Sylas took a brave step forward, calling to the Shadow Warden. 'Merida? Is that you? We just want to-'

Sylas didn't get to finish his sentence as the hand hurtled for us, and in the very next second it had wiped us both off our feet. I collided with the wall and the breath was instantly stolen from my lungs.

Blood bubbled at my lips as I spluttered in shock. I lifted my head high enough to see Sylas on the other side of the cave, also wheezing for breath. But the Shadow Warden wasn't done, it was only just getting started.

I hadn't gathered enough breath to warn Sylas as the hand came at him again. I watched in horror as it grasped his throat, sliding him up the wall of the cave until his feet were completely lifted from the floor. And then the hand threw him aside. The force of his body against the wall caused some of those sharp rocks from the ceiling to rain down. Sylas barely dodged them as they splintered the ground beside him. The shards flew into the air, and he shouted curses as they sliced at his cheeks.

I stumbled to my feet. I felt the shadow hand turn to me now. My eyes tracked down the lantern, still sat by the entrance, and I sprinted for it. I didn't know how it could help me, but I had to try. As I ran, I felt my foot catch on one of the shallow pools of water, and my ankle twisted painfully. White-hot pain shot through my body, dazing me for a moment.

And that hesitancy was all it took.

'Aurora!' Sylas yelled, but it was too late. My body was lifted by the shadows, high into the air. I jabbed my dagger into the shadowy mass but my hand went straight through it like mist.

It could touch us, but we could not harm it.

Then I was dropped and came smashing down to the ground. I fell heavily onto my arms, my head smacking the floor. My vision blackened. Something sticky trickled down my brow, into my eyes. I couldn't move. My body felt leaden with pain. A wave of nausea claimed me. Pain sung in my ears, blocking out the shouts from Sylas. I was mildly aware of the shadows slithering towards him now, picking up his body like a ragged doll once more and thrashing him about. It was going to kill us. Our dagger and sword were useless against a creature made from shadows, something we couldn't even wound.

The lantern.

That was its purpose!

I gasped as it came to me. It wasn't a weapon to fight the Shadow Warden. It was a weapon to *form* it. The golden metal gleamed at me, only a few strides away. I was so close. I knew I had seconds before the Shadow Warden finished attacking Sylas and turned its wrath to me again. I swear every inch of my body was crying out to me as I got to my feet, my vision sliding uneasily as I did so, and I stumbled towards that golden glint of hope.

Uncontrollable sobs escaped my mouth as I ran, I felt I had no control of the sounds that were coming out of me. I squinted through the blood and reached a hand for the lantern. The minute I touched it, it began to glow.

A beam of light, so intense it felt like the sun itself had been captured within the lantern. Behind me, I heard a soft groaning sound. When I turned, I saw the hand changing - shifting. The misty tendrils of shadow were beginning to harden, taking on a more tangible shape. The lantern's light was binding the shadows into a solidified form.

My triumph at making the lantern work quickly vanished as the shadows kept climbing and climbing and climbing, building into the already towering form before me. When it finished, the Shadow Warden stood twice my height. The last tendrils of darkness writhed into place, solidifying into a figure of living shadow. It was cloaked with darkness itself, and beneath that hood, two eyes stared out - blacker than the rest of its body. The colour of death. The colour of dying stars, fading into the void.

I couldn't see the rest of the face that lurked underneath the hood, and I didn't think I wanted to. The ground around the Shadow Warden darkened, as though life itself was being drained from the very earth. The pools of water stilled; their surfaces now black as night. It was a predator, and we were prey.

The Warden paused for a moment, looking down at the body which had been made physical. It stared at the long-limbed hands, the ten fingers, sharp as knives, crafted from pure shadow. Then the eyes like dying stars were on me. It pointed a finger to my pocket. To the Divinal Stone. It wanted the Stone back. I thought it might even be offering us to keep our lives in return.

My body ached. I was tired. No - *exhausted*. I didn't want to fight anymore. My hand itched to give the Stone over and to just get out of here.

But then I thought of my parents.

Their smiles. Their laughter. Their unconditional love. If it hadn't been for them, I don't think I would still be here. I might have taken my own life on one of those nights when the darkness of being an assassin consumed me entirely, leaving only thoughts of death. They were the ones to convince me I was not a monster. They loved me, so deeply, so wholeheartedly. With them, I was safe. I was never judged. I was not an assassin; I was Aurora - a daughter, not a killer.

And for them I would die before I willingly handed over the Divinal Stone.

My hand reached inside my pocket, drawing out the box. Inside, the Stone quivered with excitement.

'If you want it,' I said, tossing the box and catching it again. 'Come and get it.'

The Shadow Warden's dark eyes flashed with menace as it lunged for me. I ducked the huge arm that whipped through the air, and tumbled into a roll along the ground. I scrambled backwards as it swung around and imposed on me. A long hand reached out toward me; it was *inches* from carving out my face - when a sword slashed straight through it.

Sylas had cut the Warden's arm at the elbow. It fell to the ground with a wet squelch, black blood oozing from the wound. A ghastly moan came from the Shadow Warden's throat, as if there were a hundred different voices blending into one. It was an awful sound that made my stomach twist itself into knots.

I glanced at Sylas in pure shock, but a grinding sound of bone on bone snatched my attention back to the Shadow Warden. My mouth dropped in horror as the arm began to grow back again. As easily as lighting a candle. Indestructible.

The soulless eyes glimmered as it flexed its hands again, spreading the sharp talons for full effect.

'Shit,' I breathed. The Shadow Warden took a step forward. Sylas slid himself between us, brandishing his sword. He sliced it through the air, trying to prevent the Warden from coming any closer, but with its ability to re-grow body parts, the Warden wasn't fazed. It kept stepping closer.

The tip of Sylas's blade caught on the Warden's inky cloak, ripping the material away and exposing its body underneath. Bones encased clumps of veins and organs, and at its centre was a bare ribcage with nothing but a beating heart inside. Like a body that had been turned inside out. With the nausea already making my head swim, this sent me over the edge. I vomited to the side.

Sylas stood there - stunned - and the moment he let down his guard, the Shadow Warden swiped a hand across his sword, sending it scattering away. It took Sylas by the neck and slammed him against the wall again.

From the floor, I saw as Sylas's beautiful face turned red. He ripped at the Warden's hands that pinned him to the spot, but that only made the Warden clutch tighter.

'Merida, wait-' he gasped, trying to reason with the former Queen that was buried deep within the monster. But it was no use. Sylas's eyes locked on mine, and his mouth silently formed the word: *Run.*

I could run. I didn't know how far I would make it, especially with my injured ankle, but I could try. The Warden's focus was on Sylas, and I knew full well Sylas would try and hold out as long as he could in order to let me attempt escape.

But there was no way I was going to do that.

Sylas had already offered to sacrifice himself on behalf of me. He had held me together through every tough point in this journey. So there was no chance that I was leaving him here to die.

I shook my head, trying to clear the strands of light that danced in my vision. I put one hand on the wall to steady myself and hauled myself to my feet. I dragged myself up, trying not to collapse at the pain that throbbed through me.

I took the solid box from my pocket again.

'Oi,' I shouted, my voice reflected back to me a million times as it bounced off the cave walls. The Warden didn't remove his hand from Sylas's neck as it turned to me.

Within a split second I had hurtled the metal box at one of the sharp rock formations above the Warden's head. The spike wobbled precariously before breaking loose and whistling through the air. It plunged straight toward the Warden, forcing it to drop Sylas as it dove aside. Sylas hit the ground, slumping to the side. He didn't move.

'No!' I screamed. Sylas did not respond.

Anger seethed in me. Building steadily. I was so *bored*. Bored of being picked on.

Screwed over.

And over.

And over.

The fear drained from me. And in its place was pure fury.

Both mine and the Shadow Warden's eyes fell on the box encasing the Stone at the same time, and we both lunged. It had bounced from the spiked rocks and was much closer to me. I grabbed it, and as soon as my hand had curled around the box, the air shifted before me as a powerful hand swept across my chest. I was hauled into the wall again, my back cracking under the impact. I wheezed, trying to catch my breath. My head felt as though bolts had been screwed into it.

The Shadow Warden advanced slowly, each step deliberate, its dark form blotting out the blue gleam of the bioluminescent glow worms. Now that Sylas was down, it had just one target. In a last, desperate attempt, I grabbed my dagger and hurled it with everything I had. It sliced cleanly through the air, striking true, and lodged itself deep between the Warden's eyes.

My mouth fell open. Had I done it? Killed it?

The Shadow Warden reached a slow hand up - and pulled out the blade.

It merely cast the dagger aside and it clattered uselessly to the floor. The weapon that had saved me time and time again. But compared to the Warden - it was nothing.

The Warden stopped before me. A dark promise of death lurking above. I stared up at it from where I lay defeated against the wall, my breath coming in short wheezes that scraped against my lungs. Those cold, cold eyes were on me. But I had nothing left. It knew I was done. The fight was gone from me. I was far too injured. I looked down at the box in my hand, and then up at the Warden.

'Make it quick,' I croaked. With one finger, I drew a cross on my chest. Right above my heart. A mark. But not for me.

A hand reached through the middle of the Warden, right around the spine and through the ribcage, grabbing hold of that exposed beating heart inside. I sucked in a breath as the hand pulled, ripping the heart right out of the Warden's body.

A hollow screech ripped from the Warden's throat. Not one voice, but many, all in union as they screamed in agony. Queen Velraxis had said that Merida and her loyal followers had merged their souls to become one when they formed the Shadow Warden. So, by killing it, we hadn't just claimed one life, but several all in one go. The Warden convulsed on the spot, its talons clawing at its empty rib cage. It sank to its knees, and behind it stood Sylas - Sylas, who had only pretended to be unconscious. His face was deathly pale in comparison to the black blood that dribbled down his arms as he held onto that still pounding heart. He stared at it in a disbelieving disgust, and finally dropped it to the floor. It hit the ground with a sickening squelch.

My whole body felt tight with pain. I struggled to stand on my twisted ankle and Sylas rushed over to help me, throwing an arm around my waist. The Shadow Warden was still breathing somehow, even without its heart, but its breath rattled uneasily as I hobbled over.

I stared down at it from a safe distance as I asked coldly, 'How do we open the box?'

The Warden watched me intently.

'I will never tell you,' it hissed, its many voices blending together. 'Only one

128

with the right purpose can unravel its secret. The box resists those who act out of compulsion, greed, lust for power. It was created to defy *her*, because she could never comprehend what truly opens it.'

I sighed and turned my back on the creature. 'Come on,' I said to Sylas. 'Let's get out of here. Queen Velraxis will know how to open the box.'

A choking sound came from behind us as the Warden struggled to sit up. 'You cannot give that Stone to Queen Velraxis. It will be the worst mistake you'll ever make.'

I paused. 'Why?'

'Let's go, Aurora,' Sylas said, putting a hand on my arm. I shrugged him off.

I turned back to face the dying creature, narrowing my eyes. 'Why?' I repeated, sharper this time.

'She plans to use it for destruction,' the Warden rasped. 'She'll use that Stone to destroy everything you know.'

My heart skipped a beat. 'What do you mean?'

'Don't you know?' the Warden hissed. 'Queen Velraxis plans to use the Divinal Stone to bring down the barrier between humans and Fae. If she gets hold of it, the Veil won't just drop on the Night of Two Moons; she'll make it fall permanently.'

A slow, paralysing horror crept over me, making the back of my neck prickle.

'But- but why would she do that?'

'Why do you think?' the Warden snapped. 'So she can take over Nexonia.'

The words hit me like a blow, and it felt like I was drowning. 'No, no, you're wrong. She wants the Stone back to keep Fae power strong.'

'You have been lied to,' the Warden scoffed, shaking its head. 'It's true that the Divinal Stone will strengthen Velraxis, but she doesn't want it for the good of the Fae. She wants it to gain power over you humans.'

My head was reeling. This was all wrong.

'How do you know this?' Sylas said, his voice rough at the edges.

'When I was Queen,' the Warden continued, 'Velraxis was part of my trusted inner circle. They were there to advise me, and for me to confide in. I remember Velraxis once proposed the idea that we use the Stone to take down the Veil, and claim Nexonia as our own. She argued that as "superior beings", the humans should work for us - another way of saying they should be our slaves. I dismissed the idea immediately. I have always believed that humans and Fae should remain separate, and I was horrified she had even suggested it. Velraxis was smart, and knew better than to push the idea to me ever again, lest I remove her from my inner circle forever. But of course, after that moment, I never fully trusted her again. And now she has stolen my place on the throne, so if you give her the Divinal Stone, she'll finally have the power to put her plan into motion - the one she wanted to carry out all along, but I was in her way.'

'But why should we trust you?' I shot back. 'Velraxis told us your story, Merida - how you went mad, how you abandoned your Fae.'

The Warden blinked at that. 'I know you have no reason to believe me, especially when my followers and I now exist in such a monstrous form. But listen to me.' The Warden paused as a hacking cough possessed it. 'Velraxis has twisted my story. When the priest came to me with his visions of a monstrous creature terrorising the Fae Land, I became deeply concerned. I believed something terrible was coming for us - something that would destroy everything that was rightfully mine to protect as the Fae Queen. I had to do something, and I figured my best bet would be to prepare myself to fight this monster that was coming. So, in my desperation, I worked in secret, travelling to the Untamed Territory to create a weapon - the Binding Lantern - alongside the priest, a weapon I hoped would save us.

'Little did I realise that in creating it, I was actually creating a weapon that could be used against myself. I turned out to be the shadowy monster the priest had been envisioning. As you've seen, the Lantern's power bound my shadow form into something physical - something that could be destroyed. And I'm sure it has not escaped your notice that my creation of this weapon was far from flawless.'

'When we first touched the lantern, it took us somewhere... some other place where we could see the most terrible things happening before our eyes, as if they were real,' I whispered, shivering at the memory. The Warden was nodding.

'I poured my magic, my fears, my *everything* into making the Lantern. In doing so, my deepest terrors - of failure, of losing everything - became entwined with its magic. That is why anyone who seeks to wield the Lantern must first confront their own worst nightmare. No Fae nor human can touch it without facing the darkness within themselves.'

The Warden heaved a sigh then. 'My mistake was not being honest with my Fae, not telling them the truth about why I was travelling to the Untamed so much, and why I was abandoning my queenly duties. And yes, in some ways, I guess I did go mad. But it was only because I was obsessed with *protecting* them. Velraxis, cunningly clever as she is, used my good intentions against me. She went behind my back, spreading lies and twisting everything. She gathered support from my Fae to become the new Queen, claiming that I was unfit to rule any longer. But the true reason she wanted to take my place was so that she could access the Stone and invade Nexonia herself.'

'But what happened? Why did you turn into the Warden?'

'A few days after Velraxis had suggested we use the Stone to bring down the Veil, someone I trusted asked to meet me in the Fae Gardens - a quiet and secluded spot in our Land.' The Warden's voice softened then, as though haunted by the memory. 'And so I went alone, as promised. But as soon as I arrived, I was ambushed by Velraxis and her new followers. I cried out for help, but only a handful of my loyal Fae arrived in time. We were far outnumbered. They were killing us.

'In my desperation, I used the Stone's power to merge my soul and those of my loyal followers into this body - the Shadow Warden. The very monstrous creature the priest had been having visions of. The creature I had feared would harm my Fae turned out to be me. We sacrificed our very lives to protect the Stone and fled with it.'

My voice sounded far-away as I asked, 'And you cursed the Stone, didn't you?'

The Warden nodded. 'I believed that by ensuring no Fae could ever touch it - unless presented willingly by a human - I could stop Velraxis from accessing it until another Fae took over her place as King or Queen. I thought this was wise, as I presumed a human would only ever give the Stone to a Fae ruler who wanted peace between the Lands.'

Sylas had gone silent, his face pale. We had been lied to. Questions flooded my mind, one after another. 'Why does Velraxis need the Stone? Can't she invade when the Veil drops on the Night of Two Moons?'

The Warden exhaled a ragged breath. 'I told you. Velraxis is greedy. She wants to rule Nexonia from the comfort of her throne in the Fae Land. Why settle for a realm she can only visit for an hour once a month? No, she wants total control. And if you give her the Stone, she'll have the power to perform a ritual that will bring the Veil down forever. Then Nexonia will be hers for the taking.'

The Warden's words settled over us, leaving a ringing silence.

It was only when I mentioned Velraxis's name and revealed who the Stone was destined for that Merida - the Shadow Warden - attacked us. My heartbeat thundered in my ears.

'So if we give this Stone to Velraxis-'

'She'll make humans her slaves,' the Shadow Warden said, nodding slowly.

'But what am I supposed to do?' My heart was plummeting. 'My family is being held hostage by the human queen in Nexonia, and the only way for me to get them back is to fulfil my bargain with Velraxis - to give her the Stone. I can't let Nexonia be enslaved, but I can't let my family die!'

The Warden's shadowed eyes fixed on mine, the weight of countless souls within them.

'What is the worth of your family's lives when tens of thousands of humans will be tortured and slaughtered? You... and your family included. We sacrificed ourselves for humanity's freedom. You cannot give her the Stone.' The Warden let out a hacking cough. We all knew this was its final breath as it choked out its last words.

'Do what is right. Not what is easy.'

Chapter Eighteen

I don't know how long I had been staring at the box in my hand, but even when I closed my eyes, I could still see it. I ran my thumb over the inscription for what felt like the hundredth time. I hadn't even realised there was writing engraved on the box until we left the cave, when I finally had the time to study it properly.

Every day since then, I had been turning the riddle over in my mind, examining each word, trying to make sense of it. And every day, I traced my fingers over the box, going over each detail again and again.

'I give but get nothing in return,
Use me, burn me, light me up in flames,
I will always give without return,
I go unnoticed in the shadows,
Even if the glory was all mine,
What am I that can only give and give?'

For the life of me, I couldn't work it out. Neither could Sylas. And it was tearing me apart. Those words consumed me. And I let them, so that there was no other room in my brain for other thoughts or decisions I would need to make. I thought about the riddle day and night. Night and day.

Sylas had tried to smash the box against trees. I had tried to cut it with my dagger. We had burned it in fires. But the box would not open without the answer.

I had barely spoken to Sylas since we emerged from the cave. I mainly offered grunts or nods to any attempt at conversation. We had settled down for the night when he tried to make conversation again.

'You need to sleep, Aurora,' Sylas said quietly, as though I might break at any moment.

'As I've said a thousand times, I am not tired. I'll take the first night watch,' I snapped. He sighed, scrubbing a hand over his face.

'Maybe we should talk about it,' he coaxed.

'I don't know what you're talking about,' I said coolly. I did.

'I know how hard this burden must be for you-'

'Do you?' My glare was sharp, and Sylas squirmed under it. 'Because last I checked, you don't have any parents being held hostage. What's at stake for you?'

Hurt gleamed in his eyes, but he persisted. 'You're right. What I mean is, I understand the turmoil going on in your head right now.'

I wet my lips. 'There's no turmoil. I know what I'm going to do.' Sylas's eyes widened. 'I'm going to save my parents. I'm going to give Velraxis the Stone.'

Sylas moved closer, resting a hand on my knee. 'Aurora, I know how much you want to save your parents, but please think about this. If you give the Queen Velraxis the Stone, you'll save you parents temporarily, but they'll become slaves once she shatters the Veil.'

I pushed his hand away. 'So, you think I should let them die, then? Let them be tortured and die a horrible death at the hand of the Queen of Nexonia?'

'But isn't it worse if they live, only to suffer as slaves?' Sylas pleaded.

I was seething now. 'Alive is better than dead, Sylas! And what about the Heir - think about the civil war that'll ruin Nexonia if we don't return him alive!'

'I know. We'll need to come up with a plan. But, Aurora, we can't give the Stone to Velraxis. We can think of another way to save your parents-'

'There is no *other* way, Sylas!' I yelled. He flinched, but I didn't care. Blood boiled in my veins, fury flooding every part of me. 'If there were, believe me, I would try it. But we have two choices: we hand over the Stone so my parents and the Heir live, or we don't, and they die. I cannot - *cannot* - let my parents die. They are everything to me. So yes, I'm going to take the selfish option.

'I've spent my whole life serving that damn Queen, and for what? For her to throw it all back in my face and threaten my parent's lives. I've killed for her since I was sixteen! Sixteen! She can clean up this mess of a war with the Fae herself. I'll give her back her son, and as soon as I get my parents back, we are leaving. Getting out of Nexonia before the Fae attack. If you had any sense, you'd do the same.'

The words were flung at him, but deep down, I hoped he'd listen. That he'd escape before the Fae attacked.

He sighed, dropping his head into his hands. But I knew he wouldn't stop me from giving that Stone to Velraxis.

'Go to bed, Sylas,' I said hoarsely. 'I'm taking first watch.'

He did, reluctantly, unwilling to argue further. The burnt-out exhaustion in me that had been building since the start of our journey had disappeared, replaced by a restless, twitchy energy. I stared into that box, my foot tapping endlessly.

Once Sylas was asleep, I tended to my injuries. Overall, they were improving, but were by no means fully healed. My head wound had closed, but turning too quickly still brought a wave of nausea. I re-bound my arm; the wound was still oozing but showed no signs of serious infection, which was a relief. My ankle throbbed with pain, but the swelling had reduced significantly over the past few days, due to the makeshift crutch I'd fashioned from a tree branch to ease the pressure. Sylas had offered to carry me despite his own injuries, but I had declined. He was healing well too, but angry black bruises had blossomed along his neck where he had been strangled. But we were alive.

So why did it feel like I was dying? My heart felt so heavy in my chest. I had to save my parents. My mind was made. But the suffering I would cause...

I sat most the night, picking at my nails until they were stubs, my eyes unfocused.

When morning finally graced me from my unsuccessful attempt at sleep, Sylas and I carried out our usual routines of checking the traps we had set the night before. We had caught two rabbits today, and roasted them over the fire, eating some now and tucking most in the pack for later. We didn't speak of the fact I had lost my temper last night. In fact, we didn't speak at all. I let Sylas take control, leading us back using the Desire Compass so that I could focus on the riddle.

I just trailed behind him, wrapped up in my own misery. It was fortunate that nothing else had attempted to abduct or kidnap us, because my attention was spent. I was only snapped from the riddle's words binding themselves around my mind when I walked straight into the back of Sylas. He had stopped at the top of a steep hill and was peering at something intently. I stepped around him, scowling, and that's when I saw it. Sprawled down below.

'Is this the village-'

'Where Lumen was captured? Yes, it is. And we are going to get her back.'

When my eyes met his I found them burning with mischief, and a little hope. I dug my nails into my arms.

'What if they killed her already? And how the Veil will we get in, they will kill us on sight, Sylas.'

'Good thing I have a great plan,' he winked.

* * *

Sylas's 'great' plan was in fact idiotic and dangerous. But it was the best we had.

It was both excitement and fear that bubbled in my veins as he explained it to me. But the mission to get Lumen back was a very welcome distraction from the burdens that had been weighing me down the past few days.

I knew Sylas wasn't as attached to Lumen as I was, and if it weren't for me, I doubt he would have gone back for her. But I could tell he was desperate to rescue her now, to do something to lift the depression that had settled over me. Yet again, Sylas was putting his life at risk… for my sake.

We waited patiently until the precious cover of nightfall fell before creeping over to the wall surrounding their village. It seemed higher up close than

I remembered, stretching up into the inky-black sky above. The bottom of the wall was completely smooth, as if it had been sanded specifically to prevent anyone from climbing. But a little further up, sharp stones jutted out - potentially usable as footholds to scale the wall.

'Ready?' Sylas asked, his brow crinkled in concern. I nodded firmly. We were going to get Lumen back. He knelt on two knees before me so that I could clamber onto his shoulders. For a moment, I just stared down at him, smiling.

'You're enjoying this too much,' he said with a pretend scowl, but amusement danced in those beautiful eyes. I shrugged.

Then I placed one foot onto his shoulder, grabbing his out-stretched hands to steady myself, before placing the other one on to the other shoulder. I shuffled my weight around, trying to perfect my balance. Sylas got to his feet very slowly, I wobbled precariously but managed to stay on. I was much higher now, easily able to grab hold of two stones and wedge my foot into a crevice, stepping away from Sylas's shoulders. He backed away slowly.

'Now you,' I whispered over my shoulder. After securing my position, I lowered myself slightly by bending one leg, letting the other stretch out beneath me. Sylas sprinted toward the wall, sprang up, and grabbed hold of my outstretched leg, using it to reach the first stone and haul himself up beside me.

'Nearly tore me off the bloody wall,' I huffed.

Sylas only winked.

'I would never let you fall.'

We both scaled the wall silently, searching for good footholds and stretching to reach the jagged stones above that allowed us to climb all the way to the top. Once we reached it, I peeked over. The village was mostly empty, with most people in bed by now, though a few still milled about. We were facing the backs of their wooden houses, which would give us enough cover to slip over the wall without being spotted. From up here, I could see the stable block, its doors closed for the night, and I prayed that Lumen was tucked up inside, still alive. I didn't know if I could keep going if she weren't. Our whole plan depended on it.

Sylas went first, he swung his legs over the wall, body pressed flat against the stone, and dropped to the other side. He scanned the surroundings for a moment before beckoning to me, and I joined him, my landing making a soft thump against the mud-packed floor. We both paused, listening. Nobody came to investigate the noise. When I turned to Sylas he mouthed *'Please be careful'*. I nodded firmly and we parted ways.

Stables. I needed to get to the stables. They were on the other side of the ring of houses, and I'd have to go all the way around to stay hidden behind the cover of the buildings. There was no chance I was going to cut across the middle and risk exposing myself, even if it was the quickest option. It was much too risky. So I crept from house to house, peering between gaps as I went to ensure nobody saw me. I pushed aside the dilemma that had been tormenting me for days and focused solely on the task at hand. Every heartbeat said: *find Lumen, find Lumen, find Lumen.*

I peeked around the next house. A leering drunken laughter sounded out and I reeled back into the shadows as two men stumbled past. I was getting closer to the stables now, darting between one house, then the next, and the next. Finally, I reached the stable's back door.

I pressed my ear against the wood, listening to the sounds inside. All I could hear was soft rustling, which I could only pray came from the horses moving about inside rather than human-made sounds. There was only one way to tell - to enter.

I opened the stable door a crack to take a peek. It was gloomy, no candles lit inside. But that was a good sign that no people were about. I slipped through, closing the door behind me. My head swayed from side to side as I peered into the darkness, trying to spot Lumen. Glamoured or not, I knew she would stick out from the rest of the horses pretty easily. I couldn't stop my heart from pounding in my throat as I stuck my head into each stable, my heart faltering every time it wasn't her.

But then a soft snicker came across from me. I snapped my head over - there she was.

Quietly trying to get my attention. Unglamoured, and in her usual, beautiful form. Her intelligent eyes sparkled with relief at the sight of me and she thrashed her head silently. My eyes fell to her stable door. This was not a simple wooden one like the others, but a sturdy metal one, with multiple hooks so that she could not kick it down, even with her Fae strength.

I rushed over to her, sinking my face into her soft coat, and her long neck wrapped around my body in an embrace.

'Oh girl, thank you. You saved us!' I pulled back and placed my forehead against hers. 'And now we are going to do the same for you.'

I started as I heard shuffling footsteps making their way towards the stable. Lumen stepped back from her metal door; an invitation for me to jump into the stable with her. I vaulted the door and threw myself to the ground, scooping handfuls of hay over my body. I was hidden at a quick glance, but if anyone looked closer, they would see my flaming red hair poking out between the straw.

I held my breath as the door creaked open, footsteps echoed down the stony stable floor as someone made their way down, headed straight for us. I strained my hearing as the steps stopped right in front of Lumen's stall door. Had I been caught? Had someone noticed the small figure darting about in the shadows?

'You are a pretty one, aren't you,' a rough female voice slurred from above. A shadow fell over me as a hand reached over the stable door, stroking Lumen's muzzle. 'I'm going to sell you. And you're going to make me a *looot* of money.'

Lumen snapped her jaws at the hand, which quickly retracted. 'Nasty piece of work,' the woman muttered. I smiled to myself. Lumen's temperament reminded me of my own. The footsteps faded, and the stable door closed, taking the light with it. I still didn't move or breathe for a solid minute until I was sure we were alone again. Then I jumped up, brushing off the hay that clung to me.

'Alright, girl, I'm getting you out of here. I just need to wait for Sylas's signal-'

Screams erupted from outside, followed by the strong smell of smoke. There's the signal. I reached over and unhooked Lumen's gate, letting us both out. Her tack was sitting nearby with all the other horse's gear and

I grabbed her saddle, throwing it over her back. My fingers trembled as I worked, adjusting the stirrups. I couldn't believe what we were doing. The three of us against an entire village.

The smoke smell was growing stronger - there was no doubt their town hall, which Sylas had set alight, was badly damaged by now. Horses kicked at their stable doors, sensing the fear in the air. I paused, a slow grin spreading across my face.

I didn't hesitate for a moment as I ran from stable to stable, unbolting every single door until twenty or so horses were stampeding around the confines of the barn. I mounted Lumen and she pushed through the bodies, rearing at the front barn gates before she kicked the door down with a single blow. The scene before us lit my heart up.

Revenge.

I was correct - at the far end of the village, the town hall was engulfed in roaring flames, and thick plumes of smoke polluted the night sky. On either side of us the horses burst free, bolting into the mass of bodies pouring out from their homes and attempting to throw measly buckets of water onto the fire.

'Let's go find Sylas,' I grinned. Lumen broke into a run, and we cantered straight into the chaos. Embers danced and twirled in the sky, the flames spreading rapidly as the intense heat leapt from building to building. The place was filled with people screaming orders as the blaze grew.

A sharp bellow caught my attention. Sylas had been found, cornered by two burly men who flexed their muscles menacingly as they backed him into a wall. Without a second thought, my dagger flew straight into the first man's neck. He keeled over, and it took the second man a moment to realise where the dagger had come from. By the time he turned, Sylas's fist was already flying at his face. The man crumpled, unconscious. Sylas snatched my dagger from the man's neck and grabbed my outstretched hand, hauling himself up behind me onto Lumen.

'Nice of you to show up,' he teased into my ear.

'I thought I'd let you sweat a little before coming to your rescue,' I shot back with a grin.

Steering around the back of the houses, we avoided the panicked crowd, galloping past the town hall, which was slowly turning to black cinders beneath the raging fire.

My heart leapt as I saw the front gate, which had been left unguarded whilst the village dealt with the fire. Sylas slid from Lumen's back and fiddled with the lock as I kept watch. My heart was in my throat. I knew if they caught us, we wouldn't just get killed for this - they would make sure we were tortured. We had not only killed their elder, but set their whole village alight.

Voices grew closer. They were coming for us.

'Hurry!' I urged Sylas, resisting the urge to jump off and unlock the gate myself. His hands were trembling, but then there was a satisfying *click,* and he swung the gate open.

As soon as he mounted Lumen again, she was off. I had never seen her run so fast, not even with the hounds. I clung tight to the reins; Sylas hugged me around the middle to stay on as we galloped far away. I glanced back at the inferno we had left behind.

Dark silhouettes shook their fists at us as their village was slowly taken hostage by the all-consuming flames. I couldn't help but laugh as the cool air fanned my sweat-dampened face.

I leaned back into Sylas, feeling his chest vibrate as he laughed too. I had never felt so... free. Despite everything that had happened, and all that still might - I felt *awake.*

It served them right, for trying to take our lives.

Chapter Nineteen

E verything was wrong. Queen Velraxis had lied to us about the real reason she needed the Divinal Stone. If I gave her the Stone, all of us humans would become her slaves. And if I didn't, my parents would die. Each option was terrible.

And yet, we had just succeeded in our rescue mission. We were all alive. All of us. Lumen. Sylas. Me. And for right now, that was enough. Even though we would have to deal with some terrible consequences later, I just let it sink back to the dark corners of my mind.

Lumen didn't stop galloping until we were miles away, until the angry smoke was just a distant dark smudge in the sky. By this point, it had begun to rain heavily, and in the distance we spotted more twinkling village lights through the downpour. But none of us wanted to stop and get out of the rain. I didn't even care that I was getting drenched; the cold drops made me feel more alive. Awake. I tipped my head back, letting the rain soak my face, and closed my eyes, savouring the feeling.

As we climbed another hill, I opened my eyes to find Sylas looking down at me with a quiet smile. We reached the top, gazing over the landscape bathed in silver moonlight. My mouth went dry as I spotted Fae Land, a tiny dark-green speck in the distance. But we could see it now. In a week or so we would be there. My breathing started to quicken at the thought.

Sylas's feet landed with a squelch on the muddy floor, and I looked at him in surprise. He didn't say anything, just offered his hand to help me dismount.

'Sylas, what are you doing? We can't set up camp here, we will never get a fire going with this rain?' I said, my eyes searching the hilltop for any sign of cover. He shook his head, drops flying from the curls flopping over his eyes. He pushed his hair back with his free hand, the other still held out to me.

'We aren't setting up camp,' he wiggled his hand, and I furrowed my eyebrows as I took it. He held my waist as I dismounted Lumen.

'What are you-' He pressed a finger to my mouth.

'Dance with me,' he said.

'What?' I said, staring at him. He had gone mad. The events from the journey had caught up with him and he was losing his mind. 'But... but there's no music, Sylas?'

'We don't need any,' he smiled. 'Just listen to the raindrops.'

I examined his face, his head, to see if I could locate a trauma wound. A reason why he was acting like this all of a sudden. I didn't spot anything, so I stopped searching and decided to just humour him. So, we danced under the moonlit sky. We moved slowly, guided by the rhythm of heavy rain splattering around us. Our eyes never left each other's as we drank in the experience, knowing that this moment was perfect. In a world where everything seemed scary and uncertain, we knew that, right now, we had each other. And this time, we wouldn't be interrupted to become a sacrifice.

I had never felt this way with another person. This was different from what I felt for Cain. Stronger. The way Sylas made my heart pound steadily under my chest - the heart I was so sure had sealed itself forever after being betrayed. But it had thawed, and it had been slowly melting for a while now.

We spun slowly, revolving under the watchful eye of the moon. I took this precious time to study his face, to *really* take a deep look. He was beautiful: the light scatter of freckles across his cheeks and nose, the mischief glimmering in those dazzling eyes, the way his smile curved his cheeks.

He dipped me slightly, his lips so close to mine. If he just leant forward...

And then his foot slipped in the mud. We went tumbling down the hill, one on top of the other. The world was a blur as we rolled and rolled, eventually coming to a stop at the bottom, with me landing right on top of him. I took one look at his stunned, mud-streaked face and burst out laughing. He gazed at me with fascination.

'What?' I choked through tears as he continued to stare.

'Nothing, it's just- your laugh. I never thought I would get to hear it properly.'

I thumped him lightly on the arm, ducking my head. 'You have heard me laugh before.'

'Yes, but not like this.' Sylas's smile was radiant. 'Not so carefree.'

We both stood and I observed his clothes and hair, thick with mud. I bit my cheek but couldn't stop the bubble of laughter breaking once more.

'Hey, you laugh at me, but you should see yourself,' he smirked, flicking some mud off my nose. He lifted my chin. 'You look like you really want to kiss me now; I can see it in your eyes.'

He was teasing me, but he was right.

So, I stood on my tiptoes, took his muddy cheeks in my hands, and kissed him firmly. He sank into the kiss, gathering me in, hands moving from my waist to my hair, as if now that he had me, he could never bear to let me go.

The world narrowed to just his lips, soft at first. I drew back to look into his eyes. But he went right in for more. We connected, and he kissed me harder, with a burning passion that had been building since we'd set out on this journey. The whole world was him, this moment, this kiss. All the problems and moral dilemmas slipped soundlessly from my mind, and I let them.

I just wanted to enjoy now.

Chapter Twenty

When I awoke, it was still night, but everything was so bright. There was an orb of light, as luminous and round as the moon, close enough that I could reach out and touch it.

I got up, gently removing Sylas's hand from my waist as he slept beside me. The light was right there, a silvery-blue glow hovering mid-air, like a dense ball of mist. It cast a stunning illumination around the forest we had set up camp in. I wanted to touch it, to see what it would feel like. I stretched out my hand towards it, but it moved away. I took a step closer, grabbing for it once more, but it backed away, just out of reach. It glimmered just ahead of me. So beautiful. So mesmerising.

I took another step toward it, and once again, it moved back. This time it kept moving further back into the forest, so I followed it, past a sleeping Lumen, and deeper into the trees. Its beauty, its power, was massaging my mind. Numbing it. I just wanted to touch the orb and feel it in my hands. It was so pure, so *perfect*. I followed it further into the forest. It was like a leader, and I was the willing follower. I would go wherever it led me because it filled my heart, made me feel whole, made my head feel soft and fuzzy, numbing the painful thoughts of what I was to face when I gave the Stone to the Fae Queen.

Its gentle tendrils beckoned me further from our camp, luring me with their glow. I wanted to hold it. I quickened my pace, but it also moved faster in turn. I broke into a run, yet it stayed just out of reach, always a few steps ahead. I ran and ran, chasing that pure, beautiful light as it shimmered and danced through the night.

We came to a clearing and it stopped at the centre, and my heart racing, I reached out and finally grasped at it with my hand. And as I did, red-hot agony shot down my arm. The light disappeared, and my hand went right through it like smoke.

I blinked, my senses returning to me. The logic, my thoughts, began whirring into gear. What had just possessed me to follow this?

'Ah, such a pretty one for my collection,' a voice tinkled behind me like silver bells. I whirled around and found myself face to face with the most incredibly beautiful woman I had ever seen - the embodiment of snow. She was entirely white; ivory hair flowed down to her ankles, billowing softly in the wind like fine strands of silk. Her pearly skin showed through her sheer dress, luminous and flawless. She was breathtakingly magnetic - except for her eyes, which were the colour of frost, freezing me with a single look. My hands began to cramp, and I found I couldn't move a single finger. I tried to step back but my legs wouldn't obey. My whole body was becoming paralysed by the moment.

'What are you?' I stuttered as the cold feeling spread to my neck. She didn't say anything, but she moved closer, and I was unable to step away. My body was frozen like a statue. She flicked my nose.

'You're going to be worth some good secrets, I reckon,' she laughed softly. Such an innocent sound that didn't suit what she was saying.

It was then that I heard Sylas shouting. The woman's eyes gleamed like sunlight through an icicle. He sounded so concerned. I wanted to shout out to him to run, to get away, but my lips wouldn't move. The footsteps got louder, and Sylas came crashing into the clearing, the Desire Compass in one hand. His eyes settled on me.

'Aurora!' he cried out in relief. But his face fell as he saw the woman. And realised that I wasn't moving. At all. His face grew furious. 'What have you done to her?'

He drew his sword. The blade glittered in the moonlight. But the woman didn't flinch, didn't move from beside me. In fact, she chuckled again. If a star could laugh, it would have sounded like her.

'I wouldn't, if I were you. If I die but don't undo the curse I placed upon your lovely friend, then she will be frozen like this forever.'

'What do you want with her?' Sylas spat. 'Because I swear to the Veil, if you kill her-'

'Kill her? Oh no, you are quite mistaken!' she said, her voice honeyed. 'I don't want to kill her. I want to keep her for my collection, silly! She's too pretty to go to waste. A warrior too, no doubt.' Her eyes flicked to the small cuts and scrapes that I had acquired throughout the journey. If I was able to move, I would have shivered.

Horror dawned on Sylas's face. He studied the woman, his face growing paler by the second. 'I know what you are,' he said finally.

The woman beamed. 'Oh, do you?'

'You're a Secret Gatherer. You collect things - valuable things - from people. You don't give them their belongings back until-'

'They tell me their secrets! Yes, clever boy. But not just any secret, oh no, I want their deepest, *darkest* secret. So if you are willing to trade yours, you may have the girl back. If not, I'm going to have to ask that you hurry along now so I can take her to my collection.'

'What do you mean your collection?' Sylas's knuckles were white around the hilt of his sword.

'Oh, you should see it, my, it's beautiful! You see, some people don't think that another person, or belonging, is important enough to trade secrets for. If they don't want to give me a secret to get it back, then I take it,' she smiled sweetly.

'But why? Why do you need my secrets - how does this benefit you?' Sylas shouted, his frustration building. She seemed delighted by his anger, clacking her nails eagerly.

'Don't be foolish, boy. Secrets are *power*. I thrive on power. Secrets are what make the world go round. And we all have them, even if we hide them and pretend that we don't. So if you don't think the girl is worth your deepest secret, we'll be on our way.'

'No!' Sylas yelled, taking a step forward. 'I have got a secret. I'll tell you it.' His throat bobbed as he looked at me, holding my gaze as he said, 'I- I love her. I love her. That's my secret.'

My chest tightened. He loved me?

Love.

Never had that word sounded so beautiful coming from somebody's mouth. *I love her.*

Perhaps it was a good thing that I was frozen because my jaw would have been hanging. Sylas's cheeks were tinged pink now, and I wanted more than anything to be able to sweep him into a hug. To tell him I felt the same way. The woman only studied him with a head tilt, running a finger over her lips.

'I can sense that you are telling the truth,' she said slowly. 'But... I also sense something deeper. A darker secret.'

The blush from Sylas's face drained away in an instant. He looked... *scared.* He shook his head, his lip trembling.

'No, no- not that secret. I can't-' His voice cracked on that last word. Seeing him like this was like tearing my heart apart, piece by piece. I wish I could take his pain away. I tried to tell him with my eyes that I was here for him - that I supported him no matter what his secret was. Because I loved him.

The silver woman sighed. 'Oh well, I guess she's in my collection forever then. Farewell now!'

'No! No, wait. Please.' A tear streamed down his face, but he didn't react to it. 'You're right, I do have a darker secret. I haven't been honest with you, Aurora. I am so, *so* sorry.' He blinked furiously before taking a deep breath. This time he couldn't bring himself to look me in the eye. 'I am Fae.'

The word ripped my mind to ribbons. Fae. Fae. Fae.

He was Fae.

But how could he be? He was lying to get the Secret Gatherer to release me, right? There is no way he would have lied for this long? And why did he look like a human if this were true? And why hadn't he saved us all those times we had been ambushed if he had powers? Question after question arose in my head, but I couldn't speak any of them. None of this made any sense. All I could do was stare blankly. Another tear rolled down his cheek.

'I know what you're thinking, Aurora' he said, his voice barely audible. 'I will explain everything to you. I promise.'

The Secret Gatherer, who had been watching the events unfold with glee, snapped her fingers, and the icy bonds holding my body hostage thawed.

'Oh my, what a mess!' she sighed happily.

I could now move my fingers, my arms, my legs again. But I didn't. I only stared and stared at the man across from me, who had become a stranger in a matter of seconds.

I had thought I loved him, but in reality, I didn't even know him. My face burned at the humility of it all. Sylas approached, stumbling over his words to explain himself. Before he could touch me, I barged past him, ignoring the twinkling laugh from the Secret Gatherer. I marched straight into the forest, not even sure if this was the right direction to get back to our camp.

Trees blurred as tears stung my eyes. A small sob escaped me, and I bit my lip to stifle it. Heavy footsteps came crashing through the undergrowth behind me.

'Aurora! Aurora, please wait! Let me explain myself-'

I spun on my heel, stalking right up to him. 'I don't have to do *shit*. But sure, please do let me know at what point on this very long journey you planned on letting me know that you were *Fae?*'

'I know, I should have told you so long ago. I felt like there was no right time, we were constantly being attacked or kidnapped-'

'We have been together, side by side, for almost a month! And not once did you think to say, '*Oh hey, Aurora, by the way, I am not even human, I am actually Fae?*'

'There was no way to just slip it into conversation. Listen, I'm not making excuses, you are right, but listen-'

'I'm all ears, Sylas. Speaking of which, why *are* your ears normal? Why aren't they pointed like the rest of the Fae?'

'Because they took my powers. Queen Velraxis - she is my mother, and-'

'Your *mother?*' I spat. I barked out a hollow laugh. My head was reeling. 'She is your *mother*. This just keeps getting better and better!'

The lines of despair deepened as Sylas ran his hands over his face. One part of my heart burned with anger towards him, but the other wanted to hold him. I could feel my heart fracturing all over again - a new, fresh wound of betrayal to add to the scars of the last one.

But things were beginning to click into place the more I thought back. When Sylas had first headed into the Fae Land, I had been hit with that paralysing dread that the tales spoke about - but Sylas had been completely fine. He had worn a helmet when we spoke to Queen Velraxis, and he hadn't taken it off until we were far away from the Fae. He had never been in awe the way I had when I found out Lumen was a carnivore, or when the Fae bread filled us up with a single bite.

He opened his mouth to speak again, but I held up a hand.

'*Enough*,' I said. My shoulders slackened as I blinked at the ground. 'Enough. I can't talk about this tonight; I just- I just can't deal with all this. I already have so much to think about... I can't do it right now. Just take us back to the camp. Please.'

His shoulders dropped at the request, but he didn't challenge me. As I trailed behind him, I felt a familiar aching in my chest. Dull and hollow. As if someone had carved out my heart. I missed my parents. I missed them so badly.

And just like that, I felt more clarity than ever in my decision. To give the Fae Queen the Divinal Stone so I could rescue my parents - the only people in this world that I could trust.

As we reached the camp, we found Lumen awake. She trotted up to me as I emerged from the thick pine trees, and I pressed my face into her fur. Her body was warm and comforting. I would miss her so much when I returned to Nexonia.

It was dark still, but I knew it must not be long until dawn. I snatched the cloak Sylas and I had slept under only hours earlier and took it to a nearby tree. I nestled amongst the carpet of pine-needles littering the ground, turning my back on the image of Sylas who had his knees drawn to his ears, his head sunk into his hands.

Chapter Twenty-One

Tonight was the night of Two Moons.

Afternoon was closing in on us as we approached the village that stood before the Fae Land, the very first one we had stayed in after escaping the hounds. I had suggested we stay here for the rest of the day, waiting until it was closer to the hour the Veil would drop. That way, I wouldn't have to linger in Fae territory with the Heir once we presented Velraxis with the Stone. Even though she had made a Binding Promise not to harm me immediately after handing over it over, I didn't want to stick around and risk finding out if she had found some kind of loophole in the deal. It was crucial to hand over the Divinal Stone and get to my parents as quickly as possible, so we could pack our belongings and leave before the Veil was destroyed and the Fae crossed over.

As we reached the gate, we found the same hardy man patrolling. His eyes widened in recognition.

'Fancy seeing you both again. Cor, you both look worse for wear,' he chuckled at our faces as he cranked the gate open. I couldn't disagree with him. While our injuries had healed well from the Shadow Warden, the other stresses of the journey had taken their toll on us. We were visibly thinner than before; Sylas's cheekbones stood out sharply, and I imagined mine looked no different. We both sported matching dark circles beneath our eyes, a haunt from the practically sleepless nights we had been enduring.

'You staying for the night?' he asked.

I shook my head. 'Just here for the evening, we will depart a little while before midnight.'

'Well, enjoy your short stay,' he said, giving me a friendly nod. Sylas and I dismounted Lumen and headed toward the tavern, but a small gasp caught my attention. I turned to find an old woman hobbling towards me as fast as she could.

'Pat!' I gasped, running into her outstretched arms. She gave me a warm, flower-infused embrace, and I sank my head into her shoulder, feeling tears threatening to spill from my eyes. She drew back and cupped my face in her hands.

'How are you, love? I'm so glad to see you again.' Then her eyes roved to Sylas, who gave her an awkward wave. 'And who is this handsome one?' she asked, giving me a nudge. My smile fell.

'This is Sylas. Do you remember I told you I wasn't travelling alone? We have been journeying together. It is so lovely to see you again! How's your daughter?'

Pat's cheeks glowed. 'She just returned home yesterday! You must come and meet her.'

'I would love to,' I beamed.

Pat looked to Sylas. 'You can come along too; I'll get some food for the both of you. Tie up the pretty horse outside the tavern, and then you're coming with me. I'm cooking you both some food to put colour back into those peaky cheeks.' She pinched my face gently.

Jess was just like her mother; warm and friendly. Her hair was an even more intense red than mine, falling in tight ringlets around her face that bounced as she moved, and she had a smatter of freckles across her nose. Both her and her mother chattered to us happily as they bustled about the kitchen, concocting something that smelt nothing short of heavenly. I tried not to drool as I sat opposite Sylas at the scrubbed table, doing my best to avoid his gaze.

I knew he was still desperate to explain himself, but wouldn't until I said I was ready to hear it. If I was being truthful, I don't know if I would ever be ready. I wondered what would happen once I gave Queen Velraxis the Divinal Stone - would he choose to stay with the Fae, and if he did, what

152

would I tell the Queen of Nexonia? I would return from the mission and have to tell her that one of her most trusted guards had secretly been Fae all this time. Perhaps it would be better to tell her that he had died.

My fingers fidgeted with the box encasing the Stone in my pocket. I could only hope Queen Velraxis would accept it, even if she had to crack a riddle to get inside. Because my brain was much too exhausted to work it out myself.

Pat set a bowl in front of me. I took a deep inhale of the steam that writhed in front of my face. Saliva filled my mouth. My spoon clanked eagerly against the side of the bowl as I shovelled chunks of potato, leeks, and beef so tender it melted in my mouth.

'Did you both need somewhere to stay for the night?' Jess asked as she settled into a chair beside me.

I shook my head gratefully. 'No, but thank you. We'll be leaving a little later; we don't want to overstay our welcome.'

Pat reached over and patted my hand. 'Don't be silly. You're welcome here anytime.' My heart ached a little. A tiny part of me would have loved to stay here with her, pretending everything was okay. But I couldn't do that.

Pat continued, 'So where are you both off to now then, hm?'

There was a tense silence where Sylas and I both glanced at each other, not sure what to say. Jess looked between us, but Pat just nodded.

'I see. Well, be careful, the both of you. As you know, there are dangerous things out there. Make sure you always have each other's backs.'

I didn't say anything else as I kept spooning mouthfuls of that delightful stew. Once I was finished, I was offered seconds, which I regretfully declined. I thought it was best not to stuff myself before we entered into the Fae Land and potentially had to run for our lives again.

Pat stood suddenly and announced, 'I just need to pop out for a moment, I'm out of firewood so I need to go to the barn. I will only be about ten minutes.'

'Let me get it for you,' Sylas said, getting to his feet, but Pat was waving him to sit back down.

'No need, no need. I like the exercise; it keeps me young. Jess, would you come along with me, dear.' She raised her eyebrows at her daughter and jerked her head to the door. Jess's brows crinkled in confusion, but she didn't argue with her mother. 'You two sit tight, we won't be long.'

I caught Pat's eye before she left, and she gave me a subtle but firm nod. The door shut behind her and the house was engulfed in silence. I dropped my gaze to my fidgeting hands. Sylas only hung his head.

Finally, I sighed, bracing my hands on the table.

'Out with it,' I said. Sylas's eyes went wide as he raised his head. He searched my face, almost in disbelief. As if giving him the chance to explain himself was the most precious thing I had ever done.

'Really? Okay, which part do you want to know first?' he asked, wringing his hands.

'All of it. How you are Fae but look human? Why you live amongst us humans? Why you didn't think it was important to tell me? What your plan is once we get back to the Fae - your mother?'

Sylas blew all the air from his mouth. He had a lot of explaining to do. 'Alright. Firstly, I want to say how sorry I am that I never told you I'm Fae - or that Queen Velraxis is my mother. But I wish more than anything that she wasn't. I want *nothing* to do with her,' Sylas said, swiping a hand through the air. He took a shaky breath before continuing.

'My father really is dead - I wasn't lying about that. I grew up with just my mother. As you know from the Shadow Warden's story, my mother was part of Merida's close circle. Merida was such a great ruler, and we Fae highly respected her.

'But then one day, everything changed. It seemed as though, out of nowhere, she started to lose it. She was rarely seen anymore, and when she was, she seemed twitchy, nervous. She stopped carrying out her usual queenly duties, and our realm began to fall apart without a proper leader. None of us Fae knew what was happening - Merida never told us about the priest coming to her with these visions of a shadow monster. We never knew she had been sneaking off to the Untamed to work on a weapon that she believed would save us all. And the Fae still don't know the truth - it was only when Merida explained everything back in the cave that I finally understood what had really happened.

'After hearing her story, I get why she didn't tell us Fae what she was doing. She didn't want us to worry. But back then, we didn't know, we just thought she was losing her touch. My mother was smart. She noticed how the Fae were beginning to whisper amongst themselves, wondering why their once brilliant Queen was no longer fulfilling her responsibilities properly. And she formed a plan. She used Merida's good intentions against her, going behind her back and convincing us all that Merida wasn't a fit ruler - that she was slowly going mad with the pressure of it all. And we believed her. Even me.'

Sylas's voice was heavy with regret, but he pushed on. 'So finally hearing the real story... you can't imagine how much it crushed me - realising how badly my mother lied to me, how she manipulated me. I'd always liked Merida, but even I couldn't help believing she was failing as queen - because I didn't know the truth. Only now I do.'

He paused, his gaze dropping to the ground, and his voice became a whisper. 'It was me - the person Merida trusted - who asked her to meet in the Fae Gardens. My mother asked me to get her there alone. She said she was going to confront Merida about abandoning her duties, to demand she step down and hand over the Stone so my mother could take her place. I had no idea my mother planned to ambush her.

'When I heard Merida's shouts from the garden, I ran, along with some of her followers. When I arrived, my mother was screaming at me, claiming Merida had attacked her and demanding I help kill her. But I couldn't do that. Even though I thought Merida was no longer fit to be our leader, she didn't deserve to die. I couldn't just stand by and do nothing. So, I fought on Merida's side.'

He swallowed hard. 'But, as you know, my mother won. When Merida and her followers sacrificed themselves to protect the Stone - becoming the Shadow Warden to escape - I was left behind to face my mother's wrath.

'She was furious with me, ashamed of me. I had helped ensure she didn't get the Stone she thinks is so rightfully hers. Now I know I also ruined her plans to use the Stone to tear down the Veil and take over Nexonia. She refused to acknowledge me as her son after that. Couldn't stand the sight of me. Instead of killing me, she punished me in a way she thought worse than death. She turned me human and banished me to Nexonia. She bound me to a promise, like she did with you, that I couldn't return to my Fae form until I brought her the Divinal Stone. Now that we're giving it to her tonight, I'll finally become Fae again.'

Woah. There was a lot to process here.

'Why didn't Merida recognise you, back in the cave?' I asked. I hated the way my voice wobbled. 'And why did you kill her? Why didn't you try to explain who you were?'

'I look... different in my Fae form,' he said awkwardly. 'If Merida had looked at me closely, maybe she would've recognised me, even without my defining Fae features. But she was too focused on protecting the Stone and trying to kill us both. I went there hoping to talk to her, but she wouldn't listen. I wanted to ask her more about what Velraxis mentioned - about the priest's visions and the weapon, these were all things I had never known about. My mother didn't realise she was telling her banished son part of the real story. I wanted to understand what had really happened. But Merida just kept attacking. And when I saw she was about to kill you... there was no way I was going to let that happen.

'When she was dying, I didn't see the point in revealing myself. It wouldn't have changed anything anymore.'

'What about the other Fae? Do they know the truth? That your mother wants to bring down the Veil and take over Nexonia?'

Sylas shook his head slowly. 'No, most think Merida lost her mind and attacked my mother, and they have no idea why my mother was really trying to take Merida's place on the throne. She painted it out to be for noble reasons, to take over the duties our current Queen was failing at, but now I know the real reason. And when the Fae find out, I doubt they'd stop her. Not if she has the Divinal Stone. She'll be too powerful.'

I sighed heavily, rubbing my temples to ease the headache throbbing behind my eyes. There was something I needed to know - a question nagging at the back of my mind.

'Is that the only reason you came on this journey? To become Fae again?'

Sylas leaned forward. I dared myself to look into his beautiful eyes, which simmered with intensity as he said, 'I'm going to be completely honest with you from now on, Aurora, even if it's not what you want to hear. At first, yes. I saw this as the perfect chance to return to the Fae Land, to see my home again, even if it was just to strike a deal to save the Heir.

'When my mother offered us the deal - healing the Heir in exchange for the Divinal Stone - it felt like the Veil itself was giving me a sign. I hate my mother more than anything, even more so now that I know what a liar and manipulator she is, but I would've done anything to become Fae again.

'You'll never understand what it's like to be trapped in a body that isn't yours. It's *indescribably* uncomfortable. The vision I had when I touched the lantern… I had to watch my mother curse me into human form. But this time, it was permanent - I would have to live in a body that wasn't mine for the rest of my life.

'So yes, at the start, I wanted to fulfil my mother's bargain just to return to my normal self. Of course, she didn't realise she'd offered that chance to the son she despised because I kept my helmet on to hide my identity.'

He paused for a moment, his expression softening as he looked at me. He reached out a hand, placing it over mine. 'But everything changed. The more I got to know you, the more in awe of you I became. You're incredible, Aurora - strong, powerful. My motives shifted completely. I only wanted the Stone to help you. To help you get your parents back.

'And when I killed the Shadow Warden - Merida - and finally understood the real story… I was ashamed. Ashamed I ever believed my mother's lies about her. I swear by the Veil, I had no idea my mother planned to take over Nexonia.'

'I just can't wrap my head around it all. And the Desire Compass? You said you had no idea why there was a second needle?'

'I couldn't tell you. If I had, you'd have known I was Fae. But knowing how smart you are, I figured you'd work it out eventually.'

A heavy silence fell between us. I sniffed sharply, blinking hard to stop the stinging in my eyes. 'So, Sylas. What happens after I give this Stone to your mother? After you're Fae again?'

Sylas scrubbed a hand over his face, his shoulders tense. 'I'm going to do everything I can to stop her. Convince her, and the rest of the Fae, not to bring down the Veil.'

His expression darkened as he added, 'Not telling you has been eating me alive, Aurora. At the start of this journey, I told myself it didn't matter - you were a stranger, and I didn't owe you anything. But then my feelings for you grew, and I knew the minute I told you, whatever we had - whatever this is - would be over. So, I made the selfish choice. And I'll regret that every day of my life.'

My heart crumpled. Although I was furious with Sylas, it was clear he had been through so much. There was a lot of guilt in him after what happened with Merida, and he was trying to right a wrong. And the thought of us maybe never seeing each other again crushed me.

The door clicked and Jess and Pat shuffled in, holding a pile of logs between them. Pat observed us carefully to see whether the tension had dissipated, and smiled warmly as she spotted Sylas's hand over mine.

I had lost track of time, a quick glance out the window and I realised night had fallen now. The two moons were visible, slowly inching toward one another.

'We better be off, Pat,' I said, getting to my feet. 'Thank you for... everything. Giving me a place to stay, the food, you have been *wonderful*.'

Pat flapped a hand but pulled me into a tight hug. I could have stayed frozen like that for centuries - savouring that feeling of safety, that everything was going to work out. Sylas stuck out a hand to her, but she batted it away and drew him in for a hug too. I could see he needed it as much as I had, a warm love-filled hug before the terrors of whatever we were about to face.

I thanked Jess too, and they waved us off from their door. Pat's eyes watered as she shouted, 'Be safe and stick *together*. You always have each other!'

It was only then that I noticed a large red blanket behind her, partially covering an already generously stacked pile of firewood.

Chapter Twenty-Two

The forest spoke in whispers as we neared the Fae territory. I knew we were getting closer when that dread hit my stomach, making it churn like it had before. My legs locked up again - just for a second my thoughts started to spiral - but a gentle nudge to the back from Lumen kept me plodding forward. Sylas was unfazed by it of course, but it didn't stop him stealing guilty glances at me, as though it was his fault I was feeling this way.

Closer and closer we got. To Sylas's home.

That familiar green mist licked the floor around my boots, and up ahead I saw slender, ethereal figures weaving in and out of the trees. Before we got into full sight of them, Sylas stopped to place his helmet back on, hiding that handsome face from his evil mother until the time was right.

Sylas looked down at me, placing a firm hand either side of my shoulders.

'I am going to do *everything* I can to stop Velraxis from bringing down that Veil,' he said determinedly. 'But just in case, as soon as you get across to Nexonia and get your parents back, you must flee. Maybe if you hide at the Veil border, if my mother does end up bringing the Veil down then you can slip across the Fae Land and go to the Untamed. Find Pat and Jess.'

I nodded, unable to speak with the lump that had lodged itself in my throat. My heart felt as if it were physically being torn apart, piece by piece. A quick glance above showed me the moons synching together above our heads. The Veil was open.

Every step toward the tree palace brought a growing weight upon my shoulders. I didn't want to leave Lumen behind. I didn't want to leave Sylas either, even if he had lied to me. We had become like a family, the three of us, taking care of one another. Saving one another. And now it had all come to an end.

The tree's large leaves choked most of the moonlight above, leaving the place feeling darker and dingier than before. We rounded its wide trunk and found the same Fae guards as last time blocking the double doors. As we approached, they braced their staffs - but let them fall in surprise as they recognised us. They exchanged a glance, disbelief possessing both their faces. The humans had returned from their impossible mission.

'Tell Queen Velraxis we have arrived,' I said, with more conviction than I felt. One of the guards disappeared inside.

The air stirred with tension. Behind us, I could hear Fae gathering around to watch, hissing their surprise at one another. I clutched my hand tighter around the box that still encased the Stone. I could feel it's power thrumming again, it was vibrating with excitement. Perhaps it could feel that it was home. We waited in silence for the Fae Queen to arrive.

Once again, black mist descended the stairs before she did. Everyone fell silent immediately.

And there she was, Queen Velraxis - Sylas's horrid, lying Fae mother. Beside me Sylas stiffened. I heard the slight crack of his knuckles as he balled his fists at his side. The Queen's eyes widened ever so slightly as she took us in, those molten pits surveyed every scratch, every injury we had sustained on the journey.

'You're alive,' she drawled.

I took a step forward. 'Where is the Heir?'

Queen Velraxis clicked her tongue at my tone, but then flicked an impatient hand at the nearest guard to fetch him. When the guard returned, guiding the Heir before him, it was as if we were seeing a completely different child. This was not the sick, dying one we had arrived with. He now looked so healthy and full of life, able to walk completely unaided. The sickly paleness had been replaced by a soft pink glow in his cheeks, and his hair was no longer slick with sweat, but light and fluffy, giving him the youthful look he deserved. I let out a heavy sigh at the sight of him, releasing the silent fear that had been building within me from the very start - the fear that the Fae Queen might find a way to break our bargain and just kill him.

I crouched down and held out a hand to the Heir. 'Come, we are going to take you back to your mother,' I encouraged.

The Heir blinked at me with wide eyes, hesitantly taking a few steps forward. But then he paused at Queen Velraxis's side, gazing up at her. She gazed back with an expression that was unreadable - not friendly, but also not cold. The Heir couldn't seem to make his mind up as his eyes flicked back and forth between us.

He didn't seem afraid of her.

'Come on,' I urged, a slight edge to my voice. I came closer and reached out to grab his small, chubby hand, gently leading him away from the Fae Queen.

'Now for your end of the bargain,' she said, extending her hand expectantly. I drew the box from my pocket and the Queen's eyes narrowed on it.

'What is *that*?'

'This is the Divinal Stone, as promised. You said I had to uphold my end of the bargain by presenting it to you, and here it is. The Stone is inside the box. There's a riddle to access it, but I'm sure you'll solve it with ease. If not, just blast it with your powers - it'll probably open right up.'

The Queen ground her teeth, her lip curling. 'Give it to me.'

I stared at her out-stretched hand. I hated that I had to give it over. Hated that I was leaving Sylas with the responsibility to ensure she didn't tear down the Veil. Hated every step I took towards her when I finally placed the box in her palm.

But I had to. For my parents.

Her black-tipped nails closed around it. I had done it. My decision had been made. Queen Velraxis leant forward, her face inches from mine. Her eyes burned like the deepest depths of the Abyss, that had no beginning or end as she spat, 'Get out of my land. And *never* come back.'

I backed away from her. She raised the box to the night sky, turning it this way and that as her smile grew serpentine. I turned to Sylas. I couldn't even see his face for the last time with that helmet covering it. I couldn't even thank him for almost sacrificing himself for me. Couldn't tell him how glad I was that we met.

'Goodbye,' I whispered. I didn't dare say his name in front of his mother. Not until he was ready to reveal his identity.

He nodded, and as I moved past, hand in hand with the Heir, Sylas whispered so softly it could have been mistaken for the wind, 'I love you, Aurora.'

I couldn't stop the tears that streamed down my face as I walked away. Lumen whinnied softly, drawing my attention, but the Fae guard who had taken hold of her reins while I carried out my exchange with the Fae Queen shot me a sharp look, warning me not to come closer. I wouldn't get the chance to say a proper goodbye to her either.

So, with the Heir at my side, I led him through the Fae crowd, which parted before us. I wasn't even afraid of them any longer. Not after everything I had been through. Eyes gawked at us from all sides. I wondered how many of them would take Sylas's side when he confronted his mother with the truth.

It felt wrong to leave Sylas here even so, as though I were leaving a vital part of myself behind. The heaviness in my chest was almost too much to bear. Tears blurred my vision as I finally made my way out the crowd, and the Heir and I clambered up the mound.

As soon as we reached the top, Queen Velraxis's voice rang out behind me, echoing through the space I had just left behind. It seemed she had only just noticed Sylas still standing there after being so pre-occupied with the Stone.

'What are you still doing here, boy? Get out of my sight.'

The sharpness of her words made me halt. I needed to hear this. I ducked behind the hill, gently pulling the Heir down too. I put a finger to my lips to hush him and he copied me with a coy grin, thinking it was a game. I peeked over the top of the ridge to see Sylas standing right before the Fae Queen.

She glared at him as he reached up and extracted his helmet, shaking those dark curls free. He tipped his chin to allow his mother's hellish eyes to take him in.

'Did you miss me, Mother?' Sylas's voice was as cool and cutting as steel.

Queen Velraxis's mask of irritation shattered. Her eyebrows furrowed as she beheld him.

'Sylas,' she said, her voice carefully measured as she fought to control her expression. 'I didn't recognise you in this human form - the disgrace you are.' She waved a hand at him dismissively. 'But you have surprised me. You have helped bring the Stone back to me, it's rightful owner. Therefore, I will allow you to live amongst us once more.'

Sylas shook his head. 'I did not do this for you. You are nothing but a *liar*,' he said. Every word was laced with the pain of betrayal and anger that had simmered inside him for all these years. He turned his back on her, addressing the gathered Fae instead. 'Listen to me, all of you. We have all been deceived. All this time my mother claimed she wanted the Divinal Stone to strengthen our magic, to preserve the magic of the Fae. She said she wanted to be Queen to look after us all. But this was a lie. She wanted to become Queen so that she could be in a position of power, and inherit the Stone. She plans to use it in order to tear down the Veil between our land and the humans, to invade Nexonia and enslave its people.' He stepped closer to the gathered Fae, his voice rising. 'But we cannot let this happen! We have thrived independently for generations. Queen Merida knew this - that's why she kept us *separate*.'

Gasps and murmurs erupted amongst the Fae. The truth was out. Queen Velraxis's expression darkened.

'Oh, Sylas,' she mocked, her voice dripping with venom. 'Still so naive. After all these years punished as a human, forced to live among those filthy, worthless creatures, I thought you'd finally come to understand our superiority. But I see you've learned nothing.'

'They aren't worthless,' Sylas retorted fiercely, meeting her gaze with unflinching defiance. 'And humans aren't ours to control or enslave. Just because they don't possess power the way we do, doesn't make them less than us.'

The Queen's dark beauty warped as she seethed, 'Don't tell me you actually *like* those humans?' She paused then, her face contorting with revulsion. 'Veil above, you've caught feelings for that human girl, haven't you?'

'Do not speak of Aurora in that tone,' he said, his voice deadly now. 'And yes, I did. She's brilliant. In fact, she saved my life *multiple* times. Humans are different from us; they bear their own strengths and weaknesses. And we are better off remaining separate, as Queen Merida believed.'

The Fae Queen's face, twisted in pure disgust moments ago, now curved into a low, predatory smile. 'Merida?' she spat the name, as if keeping it on her tongue too long would poison her. 'Don't make me laugh. Merida was a *fool*. She was mad. She abandoned us to run off into the Untamed.'

'Lies!' Sylas shouted. He turned back to the crowd, his voice urgent. 'Merida never forgot any of us. And she wasn't mad - she was trying to protect us. We all know how she transformed into the Shadow Warden, but when I went to get the Divinal Stone, I was able to talk to her. She told me the real story. She was going to the Untamed to make a weapon to *protect* us from what she thought would harm us.

'Everything she did was for us, including sacrificing herself to become the Shadow Warden and take the Stone far away from my mother, so she could never bring the Veil down. My mother has twisted everything, manipulating me, manipulating all of you, to seize power for herself. She stole Merida's throne. Don't let her twist your minds now!'

I couldn't see the Fae's faces from here, but from the back, they appeared frozen in place, staring at their Queen with confusion or realisation. Or both. Queen Velraxis's ruby eyes flashed dangerously as she surveyed the damage Sylas was causing.

'Don't listen to my fool of a son. He is weak. He has been corrupted by his time amongst the humans. He does not see their true nature. They are tools, meant to serve us. They have no place beside us as equals. Nexonia is ours for the taking!'

Sylas only spoke louder to the Fae, ignoring his mother completely. 'Humans have lives, families, and friends, just like us. Who are we to take that from them just because we can? You are weak if you exploit others simply because you have the power to do so. We have thrived without slaves all this time - why should we need them now?'

Sylas's words hit a mark, and murmurs rippled through the crowd. Even from the mound, I could see the tiniest flicker of desperation in the Queen's eyes. But then it burned away, replaced by molten fury. She took a deep breath.

'How disappointing,' Queen Velraxis said calmly, silencing the crowd with two words. 'Clearly, being turned out to live as a human in Nexonia was not punishment enough. You are no son of mine. Therefore, you must die.'

The whole world collapsed in on that word. There was no air left in my lungs as the Queen beckoned for her guards to approach Sylas - to end him. Each braced their staffs, and the crowd of Fae backed away from the scene. Sylas was left alone, completely exposed as the guards prowled closer.

But something was changing.

At first, it was just his ears - shifting from human ears to become sharp and pointed. Then Sylas began to grow rapidly, shooting upward as his limbs stretched and lengthened. In a matter of moments, he was no longer looking up at the guards; instead, he stood an inch or so taller. Two ram-like horns protruded through his dark mass of hair, curling backwards like a crown, ending with a piercing spike. He looked even more beautiful, if it were possible… positively ethereal.

Beautiful, but deadly, like the glint of a dagger before it strikes true.

From the moment I handed over the Divinal Stone, Sylas's bargain with his mother was set in motion - he would return the Stone in exchange for his Fae body. The transformation must have begun as I walked away, power quietly beginning to surge back through his veins. Now, however, it was in full effect. His body was reverting to its true form, and as the change unfolded, the guards stood frozen, watching in awe.

'What are you waiting for? *Kill him!*' the Queen screeched, her voice trembling with impatience and rage.

The Fae soldiers advanced, baring their sharp teeth. The closest thrust his staff at him and I cringed - but Sylas was rapid. His strength had been magnified from his time near the Divinal Stone, and he easily snatched the staff, swinging it around to turn it back on its owner. Sylas launched it straight into the guard's head. The guard fell backwards, dead. Sylas had no time to recover from the attack as the next one came straight for him, jabbing the staff at him. Sylas rolled beneath the attempted blow, tackling the guard's legs. The guard fell to the ground in a tangle of long limbs, giving Sylas the chance to snatch his staff too, and drive it through the Fae's heart. The five guards remaining blinked at him stupidly.

'Someone kill him *now!*' the Queen seethed, pointing at her son. They circled him, each attempting to finish him off, but Sylas danced through them with deadly grace, slashing and carving through the waves, each movement steady and lethal. Blood, flesh, and vomit rained down at his feet as he fought.

Queen Velraxis's eyes darted from Fae to Fae as they fell before Sylas. As the last one fell with a piercing scream, the Queen rolled her neck. A sickening crack echoed through the space. Not a single Fae in the crowd dared to move.

'It seems,' she snarled quietly, 'that if you want something done right, you have to do it yourself.'

She handed the Divinal Stone box to the one guard remaining by her side. There was nothing but the promise of death in her eyes as she stalked towards her son.

No love.

No regret.

No compassion.

And even though Sylas was powerful - his abilities heightened by the Divinal Stone's infusion - I doubted he could rival the force his mother commanded.

Her power seemed to breathe through her very soul; she was a vessel for it. I wasn't sure Sylas could win this fight alone. I had to act. Now.

I knelt beside the Heir, gripping his tiny shoulders as I locked eyes with him. 'Listen to me,' I whispered, my voice slow and steady. 'I need you to stay here, okay? Do not move. I will be back for you in just a second.'

He blinked up at me and I didn't wait any longer before I scrambled down the mound and snuck around the back of the Fae crowd watching what was about to happen.

'You are soft. So human,' the Queen crooned as she slunk closer to Sylas. 'You should be ashamed of yourself.'

'The only thing I am ashamed of is being is your son,' Sylas retorted.

At that, the Queen lunged at him, her hands morphing into claws that slashed through the space where his face had been moments before. Dark magic curled through the air, had Sylas not stumbled backwards in time then his face would have been split down the middle. The Queen swung around, sweeping the hair veiling her face.

'I will make you regret the day you were born,' she rasped. Thrusting her hands forward, she unleashed a surge of dark matter that seemed to emanate from her core. Sylas ducked and rolled, narrowly missing that fatal blast that blundered into the tree behind, burning a hole right through it.

Sylas rubbed his palms together, summoning his strength, and drove his fists into the ground. The earth trembled, shifting beneath the Fae Queen. She leapt out of the way just as a crevasse opened up, large enough to have swallowed her - trapping but not harming her. Even now, after all the hurtful things she had said to her own son, he couldn't bring himself to kill her.

But the mercy on the Queen's side was not returned. With a flick of her wrist, she sent a powerful wind slamming Sylas against a nearby tree. He crumpled against it with a gasp, coughing as he struggled to regain his breath.

I knew I had only seconds to act. The Queen would not draw out his death for long. Moving quietly, I slipped behind the remaining Fae guard who held the Divinal Stone box. He was wholly concentrated on the fight at hand. I plucked my dagger from my boot, my fingers trembling. I had never been so nervous for a kill. If I didn't get the angle right and he fought me or cried out, I was dead.

In one swift motion, I wrapped my arm around his neck and sliced. His body jerked but I had already clamped my hand around his mouth before he could cry out, and I lowered him silently to the ground. He lay before me, his eyes fluttering grotesquely as life drained from him. I snatched the box from his spindly grasp.

'Pleasure doing business with you,' I whispered, blowing him a quick kiss.

'You have ruined everything from the moment you were born. Once I have killed you, I can finally pretend you never existed. *You waste of space,*' the Queen screamed as she pinned Sylas to the tree with nothing but her mind. Gone was her calm, indifferent exterior. Now madness - pure madness -

had taken control of her. Even from where I stood at the other end of the clearing, I could see the hurt gleaming in Sylas's eyes. He had loved and trusted his mother. He never deserved any of this.

I realised then that I didn't care he was Fae. I didn't care he had lied. I loved him regardless. And I had never got to tell him that.

I would do anything for him. Sacrifice myself, for him.

Wait.

That was the answer to the riddle.

'I give but get nothing in return,
   Use me, burn me, light me up in flames,
   I will always give without return,
   I go unnoticed in the shadows,
   Even if the glory was all mine,
   What am I that can only give and give?'
The answer was sacrifice.

Chapter Twenty-Three

I lifted the box to my lips and whispered 'Sacrifice.'

The box hissed in reply before the lid hinged open, and inside sat the Divinal Stone.

A glassy black stone that emulated power. Even I - a human - could feel the thrum of its energy coursing through my fingers as I plucked it from the box. I couldn't waste a moment more.

I ran into the centre of the clearing, where the Queen stood with her back to me, tightening her invisible grip on Sylas.

'Oi, you stupid bitch,' I yelled. Velraxis whirled in surprise. Her attention dropped from Sylas, who was released. He fell to his knees, and even though he looked utterly drained, he lifted his head to see me.

I turned to him. 'Catch.'

With my perfect aim, I sent the Stone flying across the clearing, and he caught it easily. As soon as his fists wrapped around it, I could almost *see* the immediate power of the Stone vibrating through him, his muscles twitching in response. Sylas got to his feet in the same second.

The Fae Queen was looking at me in disgust, but before she could turn around to finish Sylas off, the earth had exploded around her. Sylas wasn't playing nice anymore. Not when my life was at stake now. The Queen was sent flying backwards, her head thrown back as easily as a discarded ragdoll. She tried to get to her feet, but another blast of power sent her slamming into a tree. I revelled in the horrified look upon her face.

'*Someone get them now, or I'll kill you all!*' she screamed.

169

Her words finally struck a chord, and some Fae from the crowd began to surround me, their long fingers reaching out. Before they could touch me, Sylas unleashed a howling wind that sent them sprawling. I ran to him, and he pulled me into his arms, shielding me as the Fae scrambled to their feet and charged again.

The first attacker lunged, but Sylas swiped his hand, sending him flying - though not killing him. He was protecting us while simultaneously trying to avoid killing any Fae, knowing they were only acting under the Queen's threats.

But they kept coming - wave after relentless wave. Sylas knocked them back with powerful blasts of air, but their resolve only hardened. Through the chaos of bodies being thrown about, I noticed some preparing spears to throw. Sylas was strong, but deflecting twenty or more spears at once would be impossible. He couldn't hold them off much longer.

A sudden loud stomping shook the ground, and the sea of Fae parted as Lumen came thundering into the clearing. I released a half-sob, half-sigh at the sight of my saviour, and threw myself onto her back. Sylas rubbed his palms together once more, and punched his fist to the earth; it exploded around us. Dirt rained down. He had cleared a perfect path for Lumen to escape. She bolted through, leaping over bodies still wriggling on the ground.

The Queen's scream pierced the air, sending everyone - even the Fae - to their knees. It made my toes curl, the sound worse than nails on a chalkboard. But Lumen didn't falter; she kept galloping through the scattered Fae.

'We need to grab the Heir!' I yelled to Sylas over the chaos erupting behind us, pointing to the place where I'd left him. Lumen heaved us up and over the lip of the steep mound. The Heir was still crouched there, I held out my arms to him and scooped him up. As soon as he was sat safely in front of me, Lumen pressed on.

Her legs were a blur beneath us, while the buzz of wings and shouts began to close in on us.

'Sylas, what if they follow us through?' I cried. The Veil always remained open for a full hour, and with everything that had just unfolded with the Queen, only about half that time had passed - meaning it wouldn't close for a while yet. If we tried to run to Nexonia to escape the Fae, we would be bringing the danger directly in with us.

'I have a plan. We just need to get to the border fast so I can time this perfectly,' he shouted back. With the Divinal Stone still in his hands, he kept sending blasts of wind behind us, attempting to push back the Fae pursuing us. But those with wings had taken to the skies now, and weaved in and out of trees, gaining on us much faster than those who could only run. I clutched the Heir tightly against me; his head was buried in my arms - no doubt terrified.

My heart felt like it was going to burst from the adrenaline. If they caught us, we were so entirely *dead*. I could see the hollow tunnel of trees now, the one we had walked through when we first entered the Fae Land a month ago. We all ducked as Lumen raced beneath it. The buzzing grew more intense as the Fae entered too, only a fraction of a moment behind.

'Come on, come on, come on!' I muttered.

We were so close. I couldn't help but glance back. My heart jumped into my throat at those outstretched spindly hands only an inch from us. The Fae could fly with incredible speed. Whatever Sylas's plan was, I hoped it worked. It had to.

'Three...' he muttered under his breath. We were about to cross the border. 'Two...' Lumen neighed in pain as a Fae claw sliced her flank. 'One!'

We cleared the line of trees, crossing the border. As we dived across, Sylas squeezed the Stone in his hand, muttering under his breath. The Veil went up right behind us, singeing off the end of Lumen's tail in the process.

Sylas had used the Stone to raise the Veil - if it held the power to destroy it, then it could also reinforce it. Lumen skidded to a halt, and we all turned just in time to see a Fae that had leapt after us at the last second caught halfway between the Veil. One side of its body remained in the Fae Land, the other in Nexonia. Its face contorted in agony - a frozen mask of pain - before its body disintegrated, releasing a silent scream. Grey ash scattered on the breeze.

We all panted in the silence, not moving, not quite sure what had just happened. Adrenaline coursed through my veins. The Heir was trembling. I dismounted Lumen and pulled him into a hug, rubbing his back and murmuring comforting words. We had escaped by the skin of our teeth.

I turned to Sylas. 'What now?'

He was staring down at his palm. As he opened it up, I saw the Stone.

It was obliterated.

Thousands of tiny black shards glittered in his palm. He had expended all its power to bring the Veil up prematurely, and now it had shattered. Broken.

My heart leapt. 'If it's broken, do you think the Veil will stay up forever?'

Sylas let his shoulders rise and then drop. 'I have no idea; this has never been done before.' He ran a hand through his hair. 'My mother is powerful - she might still find a way to get it to drop somehow. But it will take her a lot of time and effort, if she manages. We might be safe. For now.'

I breathed a shaky exhale. It was an issue for another time. For now, we were all safe. The Heir was alive. We had made it through.

I set the Heir down, crouching to his level. He gazed at me with wide eyes.

'We are going home now, okay?' I said, not quite believing the words coming out of my own mouth. Home. The place I was so sure I would never return to, but would have died trying.

I stared up at the faint outline of the palace ahead. The place where this nightmare had begun. There was so much to explain to the Queen of Nexonia. I turned as a soft hand touched my arm.

'Are you okay?' Sylas asked gently. I didn't say anything, just collapsed into his arms. All the tension, the anxiety, the dread was draining from me. So what he was Fae? I know he lied to me. But I also understood why he had. And in the end, he had chosen me over everything.

It was only then that I realised, after being hurt, I had never allowed myself to love again, thinking it was a weakness. But the real weakness would be to never allow myself to love at all.

'I love you too, Sylas. Only the Veil knows how long I have been waiting to say that back.' I sighed, feeling the relief lift off my chest. 'I cannot believe we are alive.'

I felt his chest moving and I looked up suddenly, wondering if he was upset. But he was laughing. A tear of amusement ran down his face.

'I'm sorry - I just can't believe you called my mother a bitch,' he laughed.

I couldn't help but laugh too. And it felt so strange, so *weird* to laugh after everything that had happened - yet so good. Sylas pressed a kiss to my forehead.

'Let's go and get your parents back.'

He picked up the Heir and placed him on the back of Lumen and we made our way toward the palace, hand in hand. A Fae, a human assassin, the Heir to the throne, and next to us trotted Lumen, the most beautiful horse anyone had seen.

I had no idea what was going to happen next, but all I knew was, this wasn't over.

Afterword

I hope you enjoyed reading this as much as I enjoyed writing it. This was so fun for me, letting my inner child come out and create a story with monsters and creatures that fascinate me.

You can find me on BookTok; I'm currently under the username *@annalise-bookshelf*

I appreciate you reading my story more than you know. And as Aurora said, this is not the end...

Printed in Great Britain
by Amazon

58835095R00108